King Solomon's Navy

King Solomon's Navy

BY NORA BENJAMIN KUBIE

Author of JOEL

Illustrated by the author

HARPER & BROTHERS   NEW YORK

Contents

1. Jared Runs Away 1
2. King Solomon's Mines 10
3. The Judgment of Solomon 24
4. The Navy Sails for Ophir 36
5. The Great Wide Sea 44
6. Jared's Trials and Temptation 56
7. Ophir is Sighted 64
8. Jared's Adventures Ashore 73
9. The Ship Reaches Punt After Sore Trouble 83
10. Ivory, Apes, and Savages 92
11. Unfair Punishment 104
12. Shores of Africa 112
13. The Land of Gold 124
14. The Temple of the Morning Star 134
15. Mutiny 143
16. The Queen of Sheba 155
17. The Stormy Wind 165
18. A Mighty Treasure 173

v

AND KING SOLOMON made a navy of ships in Ezion-geber, which is beside Eloth, on the shore of the Red Sea, in the land of Edom.

And Hiram sent in the navy his servants, shipmen that had knowledge of the sea, with the servants of Solomon.

And they came to Ophir, and fetched from thence gold, four hundred and twenty talents, and brought it to King Solomon.

. . . .

For the king had at sea a navy of Tharshish with the navy of Hiram: once in three years came the navy of Tharshish, bringing gold, and silver, ivory, and apes, and peacocks.

—I Kings, The Old Testament

King Solomon's Navy

CHAPTER ONE

Jared Runs Away

JARED sat curled for shelter from the rain under the low, twisted branches of an old olive tree. Through the silver veil of falling water he could dimly see his flock huddled for protection and warmth round their leader, an elderly he-goat that Jared had named Navi, the prophet, because the animal bleated as if he were crying doom. If you could get Navi to do what you wanted, the rest would follow. Jared and Navi had long since come to an understanding.

Jared liked his goats better than the stupid sheep. Everything about the sheep dripped and drooped; their fleece was tasseled and matted with mud, and their heads hung low. The goats, on the other hand, watched the rain with long comical faces. The old ones were bearded like wise men, and the kids, that capered to their shepherd's piping on sunnier days, looked pleased with themselves even in the rain.

Jared shook the wet dark curls from his eyes as if he, too, were a small shaggy beast. He looked like one, soaked and miserable as he was. He pulled his reed flute from his girdle now to cheer himself and his goats with a tune, but his fingers were stiff and cold, and he could hardly hear his own

1

piping above the rushing of the rain and the water coursing down the hillside.

He played a song of King David's: "The brook of God is full of water . . ." Full of water it was indeed; King David had been a shepherd in his youth, and knew what he was talking about. Irritably, Jared put down the flute, fitted a stone to his sling and let fly at a boulder. King David too had been small for his years, but he had killed the Philistine giant Goliath with his slingshot, and later he had become the lord of all Israel, father of great King Solomon who now ruled the land. These days there were no such glorious deeds that a shepherd lad could do to win fame. King Solomon's domains, far and wide, were at peace. Jared did not pine for wars, but neither did he want to live and die a shepherd, as his father had done before him, without a glimpse of the world beyond these Judean hills. When he grew older, of course, he would be drafted into the King's service for a time, like his brother Shem. Jared wondered where Shem might be, what he was doing, and when he would be coming home again.

The sky beyond the hilltop was growing dark, twilight coming early because of the rain. Jared crawled out of his shelter, wrapped his cloak firmly about him, and prodded Navi with his staff. The black goats and the dirty, gray-white sheep began slowly to amble down the slope, baa-ing. Jared urged them on with prods and shouts. He had a big voice; when it didn't break or squeak, it was almost a man's voice.

Close by the sheepfold at the foot of the hill was his mother's dwelling place, hollowed out of the rock. Jared took his muddy sandals from his feet and stepped inside. A voice more booming than his own echoed in the low-ceilinged room. "Ho there! Is it a river monster we have, spouting water, or is it Jared the Mighty?"

Jared ran to embrace his brother; he had been spared Shem's teasing for so many moons that it had lost its sting.

"Let us have light," Shem said to his mother. "Why else did I bring you a whole cruse of oil from Jerusalem? Fill the lamp so that I can see whether the young one grew while I was cutting down the Lebanon forest."

Shem was six years older, six handbreadths higher, and at least three handbreadths broader than his brother Jared. He was ruddy-colored, with a curly blond beard and tawny hair; like Abiel, his father, the widow Mara used to say. Jared on the other hand took after his mother, Mara herself, who was small, and even now in her middle years, slender of hip and ankle. She seemed taller than she was because of the way she carried herself. She said this came from balancing the water pitcher on her shoulder, but the truth was that she was a proud woman who would neither stoop humbly nor show when she was weary. She did not want to be pitied because she was a widow woman; she had had a fine husband, and now she had two fine sons. If sometimes the labor of flocks and fields was heavy for a woman without a husband, Mara would not admit it.

Jared, like her, was brown-skinned and dark-haired; only his eyes, that slanted slightly upward, were blue, as his father's had been. His mouth was almost as wide as his nose was long. Shem said Jared had watched his goats for so many years that he'd grown to look like one, and it was sadly true that his ears were a bit big for his face, his legs spindly and awkward as a kid's. Jared felt that this was unfair; Shem had been a herdsman too before he had been drafted into the King's service, but *he* looked like a lion.

Jared stood very straight, touching the vaulted stone ceiling with his finger tips. In the lamplight his brother's shadow was giant size on the wall. "Let me see," Shem said, measuring. "A finger taller perhaps—nothing worth counting."

Shem's mockery of his size had always been a sore spot with Jared. "I'll show you how big I am!" he cried, going for Shem head first. Shem grabbed his hands and pinned them down. "Now, now, young he-goat, no butting! You must learn not to fight one twice your strength." Then, looking with disgust at the simple meal of milk curds and barley cake which Mara was setting on the table, Shem said, "How could a boy be anything but puny on such food as this? We fared better in Lebanon, I promise you."

Jared caught the hurt look in his mother's eyes as she turned to see what else she could find in the larder. "There is plenty for me to eat always," Jared said angrily.

"In Jerusalem," Shem said, "they have roasted meat and pomegranate wine every evening."

"And do not we too eat flesh at festival time?" his mother answered sharply. "Would you have us butcher our flock till there are none left to give us milk and cheese to eat, or wool for garments? And who, pray, are 'they' that live so fine? The King and his queens, perhaps, but not the people."

"Not poor people like us," Jared put in.

"You must not say that we are poor, my son," Mara rebuked him. "We live in a good dry cave dwelling, sheltered from wind and rain. We have fields and flocks and even a fig tree. And when have we ever lacked for a crust of bread?"

"I did not mean it as a complaint," Jared said.

His mother smiled at him, but her eyes and ears were all for her older son. "Tell me," she asked, "are the fine folk of the city happier than we with our simple ways?"

"How could they help it?" Shem said, wolfing down the last of his barley cake and beginning on a second piece which his mother had quietly slipped from her bowl to his. "Instead of these bare walls, they have houses of cut stone lined with cedar, rich hangings to keep out the damp, and fires in great braziers to warm them. Instead of this hard bench upon which we sit, they lie on soft cushions with servants to bring them honey cakes and spiced dates. Listen to what I saw in Jerusalem: the King has built himself a house . . ."

The widow Mara interrupted him. "I do not care about the King's house. Tell me of the Lord's house, the Great Temple which the King has built. Did you see it?"

"I saw it. It is the wonder of the world. The holy of holies, they say, is gold inside and out; there are a gold altar and golden chains before it; a table of gold and candlesticks of gold, and golden bowls and snuffers and lamps and spoons. Even the hinges on the outer door are of gold; *these* I saw myself."

"I have heard of gold, but I have never seen any," Jared said dreamily. "Is it as beautiful as they say?"

"It is yellow as butter and it gleams like a lamp in the night," Shem answered. "It is so beautiful that I had eyes for nothing else."

"Where does it all come from?"

"From the King's mines, I suppose. And from taxes and tribute. King Solomon has made Israel a power in the world. And now he is building a navy to fetch back gold direct from Ophir."

"Ophir? What is Ophir?"

"It is a place—a city or a country, I know not which—where the gold hangs from the trees and all the streets are paved with it. Some say it is on the eastern rim of the world;

others that it is in the land of Punt, which is south beyond Egypt. The King's officers, who are going up and down the land asking men to serve in the new navy, say that it is in the land of Sheba, which can be reached in two moons, more or less. But I would not go with them for all the gold of Ophir."

"Why not?"

"You have not seen the sea or you would not ask," Shem said. "At Joppa I helped unload timber that came on floats from Tyre. The sea was a terrible sight. As far as you could look, it was spitting with rage. The men of Joppa say the sea does not wish to carry the ships of men upon its back; it chews them up with teeth of rock whenever it gets a chance. To Tannin the Sea Dragon, a thirty-oared galley is but a bite."

Jared nodded understandingly. He agreed; the dry land of the world was big enough without venturing upon the deep.

Mara moved to extinguish the lamp, for it was flickering in the wind of night which blew between door and doorsill. "We must not waste your precious oil," she said to Shem fondly.

"Tomorrow," Shem said, yawning, "I'll see how the flocks have done in my absence."

"Jared worked well," Mara said. "Of course, he is young. Sometimes I was afraid for him, out on the wild hills where the jackals and lions roam. I am glad you are back, Shem. Now let us sleep; we must rise before the sun is up."

Next day Jared and Shem together took the flock to the pasture. Proudly Jared pointed out each goat and ewe and ram; not a single one had been lost to the wild beasts during all the time he had been their shepherd. "Whenever I grew too drowsy to keep a careful watch," he said, "I waked myself by playing a tune on my pipe."

"Such a toy is a help," Shem said. Jared flushed; his flute was *not* a toy!

"The old he-goat should have been slaughtered long ago," Shem went on, poking with his staff at Navi's elderly flanks.

"He is the leader of the flock!" Jared cried, both indignant and fearful of what Shem might do. "The others would not obey so readily but for Navi."

Shem grunted. "I fear this Navi, as you call him, would by now make a lean and stringy roast. I'll let him live a while longer."

All day Jared found himself choking back angry replies. Shem was now the master of the flock, for he was the elder. Jared found it very hard to bear, after months of being the man of his mother's household. He had almost forgotten how small he was, till Shem returned to remind him, both in words and by the way he towered over his brother.

The following day was no easier. Again it was raining; Shem lounged under a tree, munching bread and olives from his pouch, and ordering his younger brother every so often to circle the flock and make sure that none had strayed. Navi would see that they did not stray, but Jared could not make his brother believe this. It was only when Shem was persuaded to tell more of his adventures that Jared was allowed some moments of rest and shelter.

That night Jared could not sleep. Among other troubles, he was hungry. Shem had an appetite to match his size; now that he was home, Mara was hard put to feed the family. And of her two sons, Jared thought unhappily, Shem was the more important to the household. He could hew more wood and haul more water in less time than Jared; he could shear the sheep more skilfully; slaughter them too, without any qualms. Jared knew that Shem's return was a good thing for his mother, but he didn't see how he was going to endure Shem's patronizing ways and mockery.

Jared turned and turned again on his pallet. The straw rustled as if herds of mice were scampering in it, but no one else stirred. A caravan of thoughts marched through his head. He longed to see the things that Shem had seen: the snow-capped Lebanon mountains; the port of Joppa and the angry sea; Jerusalem, city of cities. A mighty treasure, yellow as butter and shining like the sun, swam before his eyes.

Joppa and Lebanon were far away—but Jerusalem was only a day's journey. If he went to Jerusalem and worked long and hard, he should be able to earn one small gold coin in a city where gold was so plentiful as Shem said. Enough anyhow to buy his mother some of the comforts she lacked —more than the one little cruse of oil that Shem had brought. He'd show his brother and his mother too that though he was small he was worth something. But if he waited till morning, to get Mara's permission and a blessing for the journey, she would never let him go.

He rose to his feet and fumbled in the darkness for his flute, tucked it into the folds of his girdle and tightened the girdle around his tunic of coarse brown wool. The stone floor was damp and cold against his bare feet as he tiptoed to the door and pushed it open. The rain had stopped, and a pale, watery moon made a path across the threshold to the pallet where his mother lay sleeping. She turned and sighed gently, sadly. Jared blinked back the tears. He did not intend to be gone long from home.

He tied on his sandals and stepped out into the night. For one more moment he hesitated, remembering the lions that haunted the hills, and all the unknown things in the unknown world for which he was headed. Then he moved boldly forward. Somewhere off in the dark where the animals were penned, he heard a hoarse bleating, as if Navi knew what Jared was up to and did not approve.

CHAPTER TWO

King Solomon's Mines

JARED plodded along the muddy road in the darkness for an hour or so. Then, uncertain of his direction, he sought shelter in a cave. Towards morning, voices came to him through the fog of sleep. "It is hardly more than a child," one said.

"Everything has its price," said another.

Still too drowsy to make sense of the talk, Jared half opened his eyes. He saw the bulk of rich warm cloaks and caught the gleam of heavy neck chains, but there was not enough light to make out the features of two men squatting in the cave mouth a few feet from where he lay.

"If we are to reach the caravan before it moves on, we must go soon," the first voice urged.

The other man grunted and crawled to lean over Jared. His garments smelled of stale unguents, and his scraggy beard touched Jared's face. Jared sneezed and sat up.

The man drew back, wiping his face on his sleeve. "Showers within doors as well as without," he remarked, not unpleasantly. "Good morning, young stranger; peace be with you."

"Unto you peace," Jared replied politely. He gave his

10

name and the two introduced themselves. Ab was the bearded one; the other, Heman, had a stout, red face with a nose sprouting from it like the stem of an apple.

"How does it happen that one so young is traveling alone?" Ab asked.

Jared explained that he was the son of a widow woman, that the harvest had been poor, and that he was on his way to Jerusalem hoping to earn some extra shekels through work in the city.

"Have you come far?" Ab asked.

"Quite far," Jared answered.

Ab glanced quickly at Heman, and as quickly suppressed a sly smile. "Your mother will not know where you are for many a moon then," he said. "That will be hard for her. And shekels are not so easily earned as you may think. But we may be able to help you. We too are bound for the city, and will be glad of your company along the way."

Jared did not know why he felt suspicious of these two kind elderly merchants. As they plodded along the road, they occasionally fell back a pace or two and exchanged words in low tones. But why should they not have private business to discuss? It had nothing to do with him.

At noon the road forked; Jared thought it strange when Ab claimed the narrower one was the highway to Jerusalem. They came upon no merchant caravans, not even a farmer taking his produce to market. And though Jared searched each hilltop for his first glimpse of Jerusalem's towers, only spiked cypress trees stood against the sky. It was close on sundown when Ab pointed ahead and said, "There it is."

"Where? Where?" Jared cried. He could see nothing but a cloud of dust hanging between two hills.

A snicker passed over Ab's face. "Patience, my young

friend; you will see plenty in good time," Heman said, taking
Jared's arm. Jared tried to pull away. "Would you deprive
a feeble old man of your support?" Heman said, but his
grip was far from feeble.

A big encampment lay in the valley before them. Camels
and donkeys were tethered on the outskirts. A horde of
ragged, dirty men were squatting within the circle of an
armed guard. It did not, even to Jared's unaccustomed eye,
resemble a merchant caravan.

"I will hasten to bespeak my lord Adoniram," Ab said,
quickening his pace.

Jared knew that Adoniram was the King's officer in charge
of labor gangs, both slaves and drafted freemen. Again he
tried to break from Heman's grip. "You'll stay here with
me," the man said. This time the threat was undisguised.

The captain who returned with Ab wore the elegant dress
and soft blue cloak of the King's court. Two foot soldiers
in brazen armor followed on his heels. "I could use a few
more slaves," Adoniram said, looking Jared over coolly. "How
did you come into possession of the boy?"

Ab folded his hands on his breast and bowed low. "My
lord, the boy's foster mother could no longer afford to feed
him, and she owes us a large sum of money. She was glad
enough to let us have him in payment for the debt."

At first Jared had been silent, not believing his ears, nor
understanding what was said. Now he burst out with a cry,
"That is untrue! My mother did not even see me go, and she
owes no one a penny! And even if she did, she would never
sell me!"

Ab said with a smile of false pity, "Poor lad, he thought
the woman was his real mother. How would we have come
by him if not honestly? He would hardly be far from his
village alone."

"Have you the proper documents of sale?" Adoniram asked.

Aha, Jared thought. Of course his captors had no documents.

But Heman produced a tablet from the folds of his cloak. Jared had seen him scrawling upon it during a pause in the journey, but had not seen what the letters said, nor thought much about it. Adoniram looked it over, nodded and returned it. "All seems in good order."

"No, no, he wrote it himself!" Jared cried.

"My poor boy," Adoniram said, "if these respected merchants took you by force, where are the marks of violence upon your person? I see neither scratch nor bruise; not even a torn garment." He turned again to Ab. "The boy does not appear big enough for heavy labor."

Jared twisted suddenly, lowered his head, and butted Heman in his fat protruding stomach. The man gasped and loosened his grip; Jared burst away.

The two long-legged soldiers were close behind him. They were clumsy in their heavy armor, and he might have escaped if it had not been for a staff, flung by Ab, that caught him between the legs so that he fell.

"You see, my lord, though he looks puny, he is quick and strong and wily," Heman panted, holding his stomach.

"It is an agile monkey, I admit," Adoniram said. "And the price you ask is little enough." He tossed a clinking purse to Ab, who again bowed low.

Jared squealed, "Let me go! Let me go!" struggling between the two soldiers. "Oh, my pipe!" he cried out in agony, seeing that his flute had fallen to the ground only a few inches from their heavy feet.

"And if I give you back your pipe unharmed, will you go docilely?" Adoniram said in a more kindly voice.

Jared nodded, knowing it was useless for him to struggle further. Later he hoped to convince the lord Adoniram that the merchants' story was false. For was not Solomon known for his justice, and was not Adoniram the King's captain?

But when the caravan got under way next morning, Adoniram had already ridden over the hills. Jared tried to explain to one of the overseers that he had been kidnapped. "Tell that to the King!" the man said scornfully. "He is but awaiting your presence at Jerusalem!"

"Are we then going to Jerusalem?" Jared asked.

The man laughed, pointing to the red sun rising over his left shoulder. "Since when does Jerusalem lie south, in the wilderness? The King does not even know of the existence of the slave boy Jared."

The Valley of the Wilderness was a dreary sink where nothing lived; not a blade of grass, not even the jackal or the hare. Day after day the caravan plodded onward, driven by curses and the sting of the lash. Many, many days later Jared saw from the top of a ridge a long arm of water, gleaming distantly like dull silver. A plume of yellow smoke rose from a fold of the broken gray and yellow shore. An Edomite said the smoke marked Ezion-geber, King Solomon's port town on the Red Sea.

At nightfall the slave caravan marched through the gates of a walled village ringed round with bleak, jagged mountains. Men stood in the low doorways of mud huts, staring at the newcomers. They were slave workers, dressed only in loincloths and rags, their bodies burned copper-colored by the terrible desert sun, their faces streaked with soot. Everything in the village was copper-colored, gray, or black. Sickly fumes rose above the low stone smelting furnaces; burned ore littered the ground in untidy heaps. And this was the place, Jared thought, with a sinking heart, where he was destined to remain for the period of his slavery, for six long years. It seemed like a lifetime.

After his first night in a crowded, evil-smelling hut, after a morning meal of parched corn and water, he was marched with the others to the base of a towering pyramid of rock, intricately carved, and blood-colored in the light of dawn. It was the temple of a heathen Baal, Jared thought, and turned to run; they were not going to get him to worship false gods, no matter what else they made him do. One of his comrades grabbed him and pointed to the summit of the rock where two guards stood against the yellow morning sky, ready to plunge their spears into any slave that attempted to escape.

Jared saw now that wind and weather had carved out the huge wrinkled columns and ledges of the rock before him. Blocks of blue-green ore were jumbled at the base. Jared picked up a fragment and examined the veins of glittering metal running through the stone. "Gold?" he whispered to one of the other slaves.

"Gold!" the man repeated scornfully. "Does not all the world know that the mines of Edom in which we wear our lives away bring forth only copper?"

A tunnel led down through a low opening into the heart of the earth. Because of his size, Jared was put to work in the deepest part of the mine, where the passage narrowed and ended. Here, in crevices too small to admit larger workers, he crawled with his hammer and chisel, chipping ore and passing it back to the others. A lighted saucer of oil perched in a niche on the wall was the only light.

Often, in the weeks that followed, Jared let the hammer fall from his sweat-slippery hand and started backing out, like an animal in a trap. "I'll die if I stay here longer," he cried. But an older miner grabbed him and held him fast before Zedek, the overseer, could discover what had happened. "You'll die if you disobey," he was told. Jared didn't think there was much choice. Each season many of the slaves collapsed from heat and exhaustion.

Escape from the village was impossible. The huts in which the workers lived were surrounded by a thick wall with towers guarding the only entrance. The gate was kept locked and barred, and was opened twice each day, to let the workers go out in the morning and to imprison them again at night. The village itself was almost as hot as the mine shaft. It lay in a funnel of the hills so that the wind could act as a bellows for the smelting furnaces. The wind came from the desert, a feverish breath that brought sand which got into everything: food, drink, sleeping quarters. When a real sandstorm blew up, there was nothing to do but lie low with a rag of clothing draped over nose and mouth.

"You've seen nothing till you've lived through the samoon," an Edomite told Jared.

"What is the samoon?" Jared asked.

"He is the king of all sandstorms," the Edomite answered. "He roars like a lion; he pounces more swiftly than a bird of prey; his breath scorches and suffocates. If you breathe even one puff of it, you will surely die."

"How does anyone live then, when the samoon comes?" Jared asked.

"There is only one way. You can see the samoon coming from afar, for he is purple-colored and a hundred hand-breadths wide. And he does not like the earth; he comes no closer to it than the height of a man. So you must fling yourself flat, wherever you are. Thus he passes over you without doing you harm."

"The height of a man . . ." Jared repeated slowly. How often he had been mocked, told he'd never grow to be the height of a real man. Long ago he had learned that he must make up for his lack of size and strength by being clever. He closed his eyes now and pretended to sleep, trying to figure out how he could turn the king of sandstorms to his advantage if it came.

Each week the sandstorms were worse. Each day the sun was more fiery. In the mine shaft more and more of the men fainted and were dragged out senseless. Surely, Jared thought, King Solomon could not know how his miners suffered.

One day when the men came up out of the mine, the eastern sky was a murky red. The sun, slanting low, was veiled in violet. No breath of wind stirred. The air lay on the shoulders like a weight of ore. Even the effort of shuffling slowly along the path to the village made the sweat start.

The Edomites whispered among themselves. The samoon was coming, they said. Zedek too smelled the storm and hurried the gang along with his whip. Jared tried to hold back, and the whip raised a welt on his bare shoulders.

The village walls were in sight when, with the shrieking and howling of twenty demons, the samoon whirled out of the desert. It came like a djin, like purple smoke pouring from the mouth of a giant bottle. The scanty leaves of an acacia tree were tossed by handfuls into the air till, with a loud crack, the tree itself split apart and the branches soared away, light as thistle silk before the wind.

"Down! Down!" cried Zedek the overseer. "Fall on your faces for your lives!"

The men threw themselves into a frantic heap, each one trying to burrow under his fellow for protection from the stinging sand. Jared, frightened as he was, lay at the edge of the wriggling bodies, touching none.

He lay quite still till the samoon screamed directly over-head. Sheltering his face behind his hands, he opened his eyes to a squint. Day had become night. The guards and overseers lay with buried faces, garments flung over their heads. He got to his knees and began to crawl away.

But crawling was not fast enough, for the samoon would soon be gone as swiftly as it had come. Jared stood up and ran with his arms before his face. The sand was like a swarm of hornets on his body and limbs. His hair was singed by the blast. He stumbled against a big boulder, felt his way round, and threw himself down behind it.

The air passed over his body like a hot iron, and the voice of the samoon grew fainter and fainter, till with a wail of farewell, it fled back to the wilderness. Jared lay hidden by his boulder, stifling the gasps that sounded so loud in the new stillness. His throat was on fire, his mouth filled with grit. He lay for a long time before he had strength to roll over and look out from his hiding place.

Where the others had been there was nothing but tracks in the new drifts leading toward the gate of the village. Sand had covered his own footprints. For the moment he was safe.

But what was he to do now; where could he go? Through swollen eyes he saw before him a dirt-colored waste stretch-ing away to cruel red mountains and black basalt cliffs. He had no food or water and already his thirst was terrible. As far as the eye could see, the only sign of human life was the slave village. If he returned there he would get a beating, but also shelter, water, and food to keep him alive.

And yet, thirsty, sand-scorched, and frightened as he was, Jared knew for the first time in months what it was to have freedom. He could not give this up as soon as he had found it. There was one possible place of refuge. Soon it would be dark enough to slip by the walls of the village unseen and follow a road which was used to take the copper ore to Ezion-geber.

The road was a rutted track only a little more bare and free of rocks than the desert on either side. Jared followed it by the feel of his bare toes, and more than once, at a sudden sound, left it to fling himself flat. But the sounds were only the wind crackling in the thorn bushes. The wind, after sunset, was cool and brought with it a damp, salty smell. Jared spied the pale gleam of water far ahead beyond the sand dunes. He broke into a run, for his thirst was almost unbearable.

But it was no pond to which he came; it was far too big —he could not see an end to it. It was the Mighty Deep at last, Tannin the Sea Dragon, that rolled under the whole earth and washed the feet of the hills. Jared saw flashes of white on the black water; the monster was baring his teeth. But he heard only a soft drowsy sighing. An odor of decay came from the shore; his feet crunched on the brittle bones of small dead sea creatures.

His throat was dust-dry, his tongue swollen in his mouth. The lapping ripples looked no more dangerous than a stream in Judah in the rainy season. Cautious and slow, he advanced till a cool and soothing wetness laved his feet. He knelt, splashed his face and neck, then lifted water in his cupped hands and took a long swallow. He spat it out, coughing,

with his eyes streaming tears. He had, of course, heard that
the sea was salt, but since salt was good seasoning in food,
he had not expected this bitter poison. Blowing his nose
he thought, truly the sea was treacherous.

More parched than ever he trudged on till he saw a yellow
glow in the night sky. Above the watchtowers of Ezion-geber
rose wisps of smoke from the copper refineries; the smell
of charcoal fires and sulfur fumes was stronger than the salt
sea smell. It was very late and the gates were locked, but
just outside was a cistern of fresh water from which he
drank greedily. The night air had grown cold, and Jared
was clothed in a tunic so full of holes that it hardly covered
his nakedness, girdled by a threadbare rag into which his
shepherd's pipe was carefully tucked. He shivered in the
night wind, but he was too tired to search further for shelter.
Careful to keep a good distance from the sea itself, he bur-
rowed a bed in the sand of the beach which still kept some
of its noontime heat.

In the morning a thousand arrows of light woke him. A
lip of foam, wet and cold, was licking at his bare toes. He
jumped up and scurried away, fearing the sea would follow
to gobble him up. But it seemed to have no further interest
in him. The treacherous deep was beautiful as Eve herself
this morning; the gulf of Ezion-geber was bluer than the
bluest turquoise and glittered in the sun as if it were
powdered with diamonds.

Floating in the blue were four ships shaped like crescent
moons. Each had a high prow and a high stern, underneath
which a landing ladder was slung. Amidships each sprouted
a mast taller than the tallest cypress tree in Judah, and from
the top of each mast a pennant of royal purple streamed in
the breeze of morning. Jared had never before seen a ship,

but he knew this must be the navy King Solomon had been building which was soon to seek the gold of Ophir.

Jared's brother Shem had said, "You won't get me to risk my life in a cockleshell—not for all the gold in Ophir!" Jared agreed with him now more than ever, for these ships looked very small and fragile in the wide sweep of the gulf.

The glare of sun on water made him blink; he looked away and saw that the beach was littered with creatures the sea had spat up to die: slimy worms, spiny things and horned things; fleshy creatures with crowns of wriggling tentacles; dead red spiders of giant size with saw-toothed claws made to nip and pinch. They had neither fins nor scales like good lake fish, and you had only to smell them to know that they were unclean.

But nothing could be more unclean than Jared was himself this morning. Each day he had spent in the mining village had covered him with a new layer of copper-colored dust, and there had been scarcely enough water for drinking, let alone bathing.

"I must wash myself at the cistern," he thought, "for truly I am disgusting in the sight of God."

The gates of the city were open and the women were coming out carrying pitchers on their shoulders to fill at the well. Jared greeted one and asked if she would pour water for him.

"You are new come to Ezion-geber," she remarked.

"I reached here last night, but it was late and I could not enter," Jared said. "I am a worker in metals and seek to ply my trade in your city." He was sure the woman would not believe a word of the story, for he was too young to be a master craftsman, nor would such a one be dressed in rags.

Besides which no one could reach this desert and sea-bound
city alone, on foot, without beast of burden or caravan.

Yet after the woman had given him drink, and poured
water for him to wash hands and feet, she answered him
courteously, "It shames me that you had to sleep on the
strand. Even had you come earlier, we could scarcely have
found a bed for you, because since King Solomon is here,
our doors are filled to bursting."

"The King is at Ezion-geber?" Jared cried.

"Why yes, didn't you know? That is the reason the town
is so crowded. Many hope to share in the tasks of the royal
train and to be well paid for it. Then of course all the shipmen who are to sail tomorrow are quartered among us.
King Solomon has come here to see the departure of his
navy." She pointed to an oasis that made a feathery green
patch on the slope of a hill above the town. "His tents are
pitched there under the palm trees, where it is cooler than
in our busy streets. Today all Ezion-geber makes holiday in
his honor."

Jared scrubbed himself as clean as he could, thanked
the woman and slipped inside the gate to join the crowds
that were already surging through the narrow alleys. Ezion-
geber had been built for trade and manufactures, not for
beauty or comfort. No trees shaded its dusty streets; no grass
or flowers brightened its mud-brick courtyards. All of the
town was baked as hard and brown as an overdone bread
cake. The air was close and smelled of burning ore, rotting
fish, and too many people crowded into small hovels. But
Jared, who had never seen anything bigger than his mountain village, gaped at the booths selling copper fishhooks,
lances, and spearheads; at the weavers fashioning fishnets;
at the mounds of earthenware in the Street of the Potters.

The townspeople had put on their best garments in honor of the King: tunics of white linen, cloaks colored with red, blue, and green Tyrian dyes. They sauntered along in the shadow of the house walls, pausing now and then to buy a tidbit from the stalls heaped with dried raisins, dates, and sweet cakes. Jared was so hungry that he was glad to be taken for a beggar and handed scraps of food.

Two men were arguing hotly in the doorway of a shop. "Very well then," the one said, turning to go. "If you will not listen to reason, I will bring the matter up before the Court of Justice this noon. The King shall choose between us."

An idea leaped into Jared's mind. He too would attend the Court of Justice. He would tell his story to the King. Was not Solomon known over the whole world for his wisdom?

CHAPTER THREE

The Judgment of Solomon

THE crowds were beginning to push out through the gates to the oasis on the hill. Jared let himself be carried along with the stream, glad for once that he was short enough to escape notice. By now the mine overseers must surely have missed him. He could think of no way to disguise himself. He had no henna with which to bleach his hair; he could not change the shape of his face; he was not even old enough to grow a beard. The best he could do was to pull the tangled black curls low over his pointed ears and to squint so that his blue eyes, unusual in one so dark as he, would go unnoticed.

Luckily the people of Ezion-geber were lost in amazement over the King's camp and they paid no attention to anything else. Even Jared forgot his own peril in the wonder of what he saw.

First there was the army bivouac: the King's Host, encircling the whole oasis. Soldiers not on duty as guards sprawled on the ground beside the smoldering cook-fires, among the baggage wagons and the stacked spears. Pack asses, camels, and horses browsed in the grass bordering a spring. Jared had never seen horses before, for these animals had only recently been imported from Egypt to draw King Solomon's war chariots. He stared fascinated at the sleek coats, small sharp ears, and flowing manes, so different from the mules and donkeys to which he was accustomed.

In the shadow of the palm trees the tents of the King and the Captain of his Host had been put up. The tents were of black goatskin, like those of any wandering herdsmen, but when messengers passed in and out, Jared caught a glimpse of the furnishings: red and purple draperies, soft embroidered cushions. Curtains of white linen were stretched above the tents for additional shade, making a striped pattern of sunlight and shadow that shifted and trembled as they bellied in the desert wind.

Retainers were sprinkling water by the handful to lay the dust about the King's tent, and laying down a crimson carpet before the entrance. A massive chair inlaid with ivory, red rubies, green emeralds and black onyx awaited the royal presence. The back and arms were ornamented with carved lions' heads and eagles in yellow shining metal. So Jared had his first sight of gold. It was not, he thought, much more beautiful than copper. But of course it was more valuable.

Jared's presence in the crowd went quite unnoticed as the townfolk pointed out to one another each item, chattering loud enough to drown the rustle of the palm fronds. They waited impatiently, turning their faces up to the sky to see if the sun had not yet reached the zenith. Jared saw with relief that none of the mine overseers were among them, nor were any of the mine guards among the soldiers who stood in stiff ranks on either side of the throne with Benaiah, Captain of the Host, in flashing brass armor at their head. Two tall captains lifted the flaps of the King's

tent. It was noon. The trumpeters raised their rams' horns,
making the hills echo with a roaring as of lions. The crowd
hushed; Jared hid his face, but others bolder than he rushed
forward to lay their cloaks where the King's feet would
tread upon them.

When Solomon appeared in the tent opening, his people
fell upon their faces. Both the sound and the look of it was
like a storm wind passing over a cornfield, bowing every
head. The King ordered them to rise. As he lifted his arms
in greeting, motes of light danced from his jeweled fingers
and from the polished gold bracelets that reached from wrist
to elbow. His purple robe was gold embroidered; gold dust
powdered his oiled hair and beard.

Jared dared not look full upon the imperial face. With
downcast eyes he listened to the cases called for judgment.
They were disputes over debts, property rights, and the
like; he could not make head nor tail of them, nor understand
why these richly dressed merchants bickered over differ-
ences of a few silver shekels. The King had only to put a
question or two before he settled each case. And none, even
those who complained at the King's own taxes, dared make
a second appeal. Behind the throne stood Ahijah, the scribe,
inscribing the judgments with a pointed tool on tablets of
clay.

Jared looked down at himself, at the soiled rags hardly
covering his nakedness, at the lean limbs mottled with
scrapes and bruises, at his dusty, unwashed feet. How could
such a one as he dare to address the King? Better to remain
hidden in the crowd and later seek help in the humbler
houses of the town, among people more like himself.

At this moment a stout little yellow-green bird lighted
on the tip of the spear planted in the ground by the King's

throne. Impudent and unafraid, it opened its tiny beak and warbled a few sweet notes. Solomon smiled, held up his jeweled hand for silence so he could listen to the song. His lips moved, but what he said was too low for any but the bird to understand. The creature flirted its wings with a satisfied air and darted off into the blue sky.

"So may even the weakest and smallest of his subjects reach the King's ear," Solomon said in a voice that all could hear.

A murmur of wonder rose from the crowd although they had been told that Solomon knew the languages of the birds and beasts.

Jared took heart. He wormed his way forward to the front ranks. As he still hesitated to approach the throne, a shout from the rear filled him with terror.

"Seize that boy!" cried Zedek the overseer, knocking people from his path right and left.

Jared ran to the feet of the King and flung himself down, clutching the hem of the royal robe.

Zedek, close on his heels, grabbed Jared by the shoulder and jerked him to his feet. "It is a slave escaped from the King's mines," the overseer panted, bowing low. "Let me remove him from my lord's sight."

"Wait," said Solomon, holding up his hand as he had done for the bird. "None who come to me, no matter how humble, shall be taken away without a hearing. Let the boy speak to me on his own behalf."

Jared, terribly alone and afraid, looked full on the King's face at last. The noble brow was furrowed with lines of care and sadness, but tiny lines radiating from the corners of the piercing eyes spoke of kindness and humor. Jared took a

deep breath and, determined to get in his whole story before Zedek could interrupt him, declaimed:

"My name is Jared, son of Abiel, of the tribe of Judah. I am freeborn, taken against my will by dishonest men who told false stories and sold me as a slave to the King's officers, who brought me from my homeland and put me to work in the mines from which I ran away to seek the King's justice." He spoke the long sentence so fast for fear of interruption that he panted at the end of it like a spent runner.

A smile tugged at the corner of the King's mouth, half concealed by his beard. "Is this the truth?" he asked Zedek.

"How might your servant know?" said Zedek, in a tone that implied he knew very well that Jared was lying. "The boy came to us in a slave caravan. How can he claim that he is not a slave?"

"Indeed, I am not!" Jared cried.

Zedek was the hardest taskmaster at the mine camp, known for his foul mouth and rough behavior. Now he bowed before the King and said in a voice oozing respect, "My lord knows that if we believed every rascal who said he was falsely taken, we should have none left to work the King's mines."

Solomon nodded, looking again on Jared. By a great effort Jared returned the stare so that the King might look into his heart and see that he was not dissembling. Surely one who understood the language of the birds would be able at a glance to tell the difference between a liar and one who spoke true.

"Your speech is indeed that of a Hebrew from Judah," Solomon said. "Do you not know that the wealth of the mines goes to increase the glory of God, and to defend the kingdom against the enemies of God? The Lord God Eternal,

Yahveh, is your God and my kingdom is your kingdom. A king but rules for the good of his subjects. Why then do you refuse to work in my mines?"

Jared hung his head, but in that head the questions pressed for an answer and had to be spoken aloud. "Must I be a *slave* for the good of my kingdom? Must I toil in dark caverns all the days of my youth and perhaps die before I am old? Does the Lord demand this?" He faltered, and added humbly, "I seek to learn from wise Solomon the reasons for such a hard fate."

"There are slaves in all the lands of the earth," Solomon said. "In the land of Israel only are the years of a bondsman's service limited to six. You will go free in the seventh year. And there are many laws to protect the bondsman, for we Hebrews remember that once we too were slaves in Egypt. In what other country can you find such justice?"

"I only know that no man wishes to be a slave," Jared said stubbornly. Behind him he could hear the crowd buzzing like bees, whether agreeing with him or shocked by his boldness he could not tell.

The King motioned for silence, and when Jared looked again, he saw that the furrows in the royal brow had deepened. "Perhaps someday," Solomon said, "the Lord our God will reveal how we may dig His riches from out of the earth without so much of toil and suffering, without slavery for any of human kind. That blessed day has not yet come. Wealth is needed to carry on the kingdom. Men must work to provide this wealth. If the work is of such a difficult nature that no free man will undertake it, then it must be done by slaves." He sighed, and it seemed to Jared that the royal shoulders sagged as if the weight of the kingdom weighed more heavily than the gold-encrusted royal robe.

Zedek again stepped forward. His hand fell hard and rough on Jared's thin shoulder. "The boy is a slave because he was sold in payment of a debt, and he is bound by the terms of the sale whether he was once a freeborn son of the tribe of Judah, or no. My lord is far too patient and gentle with this brash youth. Let me make an end to his bold affronts to the majesty of the King."

"It is indeed the law that unpaid debts must be fulfiled in years of labor," Solomon sternly reminded Jared.

"But there was no debt!" Jared pleaded. "What can I do to make my lord know this too is a falsehood?"

The King stroked his beard, looking Jared up and down from head to foot. Perhaps in spite of the dirt and rags, he liked what he saw, a slight, wiry body, somewhat small for fourteen summers but held very erect; a head of unruly black curls, blue eyes that were alert but without guile. Again the King's voice grew mild. "You have heard that I am fond of riddles. I will propose one to you now, and my judgment in this case will depend upon whether you find the right answer to it. Is this agreed?"

"It is agreed," Jared said.

"The riddle is this: how may a slave prove that he is no slave?"

How indeed? Jared's sweat of fear pricked him like stinging nettles. How did he differ from the others at the mines, the Edomites and Canaanites? They too had once been free men. They looked very little different, were no more stupid, smelled no worse than he did at this moment. If size of body or noble carriage was proof of being a freeman, he had no proof to offer.

"Come now, my brave young man," said the King. "Have

you no more to say? Have you come to the end of your
eloquence?"

Jared, casting around wildly for an idea, saw the eyes of
the crowd upon him. There was scorn in some faces, pity in
others, but not in any face the bright eager light of an
answer. On Zedek's face was a cruel grin which matched
the whip in his hand. The only sounds were the banners
flapping in the wind as if they too wished to be free.

"If—" Jared began. There was an idea scratching at the
back of his head but he couldn't seem to drag it out into the
open.

"Yes, yes, speak on—"

"If a man will do any labor, no matter how hard it is,"
Jared stammered, "no matter how—how full of danger—or
how unpleasant, so long as he is not a slave."

"What may this prove?" Solomon asked.

"It proves that he is not lazy or a coward; it is not the
labor that he hates, but the slavery." Jared's voice became
stronger as he grew sure of what he said. "Being free makes
all the difference in life to him."

Long minutes seemed to pass before the King made a
reply. "Truly, an excellent answer," King Solomon said then.
"Even so, words are easier than deeds. Now tell me this:
what hard and dangerous work would *you* be willing to
undertake for me—as a freeman—to prove that you are no
slave at heart?"

Again Jared looked wildly around him. The hardest labor
he could think of was in the mines, and there he did not
wish to return, free or slave. He must think of something
dangerous instead. He saw the soldiers in their glittering
armor, but the kingdom was at peace; their lives held little
chance of danger. Life was safe enough in the booths and
manufactures of Ezion-geber. Beyond the low sheds of the

"Yes, my lord."

"Have the goods of Israel been brought aboard the vessels? Are the shipmen at their posts?"

"Not yet, my lord. The shipyard workers have not done with the cordage and rigging of the vessels, and the shipmen are meanwhile spending their last hours with wives and sweethearts in the town. The ships will be beached on the rising tide of morning, and then the loading will begin."

"Very well. These slaves will carry the casket of gifts to the beach. Guard it with your life."

"I will ferry it to my own ship and place it on board myself. I will secrete it so that no thieving hands will be tempted to molest its precious contents."

Solomon gave the shipmaster a long hard stare. "Of thievery among my own shipmen I have no fear. See that your servants are as trustworthy—and that *you* give measure for measure honestly in trade, Merbal. I want none of your sly Zidonian tricks practiced in *my* navy."

"It shall be done as you wish in all things," the shipmaster said.

"Then farewell and may the Lord watch over your venture," Solomon said. "Take the boy with you now."

Jared humbly and gratefully kissed the hem of the King's robe before he marched off in the wake of the shipmaster and the slaves carrying the casket. From the descending pathway he could see how the blue gulf stretched away and away and away, and how the red mountains of the far shore of Midian dwindled to nothingness, till the sky met the edge of the sea. He was afraid, but he was also happy. He was free. His heart lifted as the purple ensigns on the ships' mastheads lifted in the sea wind.

CHAPTER FOUR

The Navy Sails for Ophir

WEARY and, now that the hour of departure had come, more frightened than he would admit, Jared crouched beside one of the wine and water jars that were lashed amidships. Earlier in the day he had helped push the galley out from the beach, and before that he had been kept busy with the other members of the crew, stowing supplies and cargo. He had carried aboard sacks of meal and parched corn, and as much fresh foodstuff as would not spoil in the heat before it could be used. The huge reserve jars of drinking water were placed on either side of the keelson, under the oarsmen's feet, to act as ballast. Forward of the rowing benches, below decks, was the space for cargo: bars of copper and copper implements, jars of honey and olive oil, lengths of cloth brightly colored with Tyrian dyes, trinkets and baubles of glass with which to trade with savages of far countries. A few weapons were stowed there also, though this navy was not bound on a voyage of conquest, but upon a peaceful trading venture.

True to his word, Merbal must have hidden the casket of gifts for the Queen of Sheba behind other bales and chests before the loading was begun by the crew, for there was no sign of it. The King's slaves who had carried it aboard had long since departed, and no one on the ship knew of the casket's existence save Jared and the shipmaster. Though Jared knew the gifts must be of great value, he thought Merbal was unduly suspicious to be so secretive; none of the ruddy-faced, laughing young shipmen had the look of thieves.

High up above the deck, on the yardarm, sat the lookout, holding to the mast with one hand, shading his eyes from the sun-dazzle with the other. On the prow crouched a shipman with a sounding line. And in the stern Merbal the shipmaster stood, bellowing orders.

The Phoenician language was much like the Hebrew, but for all Jared could understand, Merbal's directions might as well have been in a foreign tongue. The sailors, who were both Hebrews and Phoenicians—men of Tyre and Zidon—understood well enough. Scurrying about in their neat white and green tunics, they cast off lines, pulled on others, in a scene that looked to Jared like complete confusion. The round anchors of chipped stone had been trundled up a plank gangway while the ship still rested on the beach, and now, Jared gathered, the vessel was being freed somehow from other harness that held it tethered to the shore. The helmsman, whose bronzed face was still that of a young man in spite of his close-cropped gray hair, sat on the raised poop deck, steadying the two big steering oars.

The shipmaster saluted the shore where the King and his captains sat under a purple canopy, waiting to see the sailing of the fleet. Merbal shouted a command below decks and the oars, fifteen to a side, dipped and flashed wet in the sun. Not far distant, the other galleys were also getting underway. A cheer rose from the throng of townspeople on the beach as the four great ships moved out into the gulf and pointed their beaked prows southward. Merbal's ship was in the lead.

The galley trembled as the oars pushed it along, leaving a long trail of foam where it broke the blue. The water made a murmuring along the sides as if sea voices were complaining. The shipmaster shouted a fresh set of orders. With a cuff and a mutter about ignorant lubbers that got in the way, Kalab, a brawny red-bearded Zidonian, sent Jared reeling from his refuge. The square linen sail of Tyrian purple was loosed from the yardarm, flapping and slapping till the shipmen trimmed it in with ropes fastened to the lower corners. And suddenly, as the sail filled with wind, the galley reeled so that Jared slid across the deck and had to grab the bulwark with both hands in order not to be spilled out.

"*Mekada* is a tender ship, it seems," remarked a sailor.

"Ay, she is built for swiftness," answered the helmsman; "she answers to the steering oars like a tender-mouthed mare. Yet she is sturdy too; I can feel that already. A true ship of Tharshish, strong enough to sail to the faraway lands."

The galley righted itself and began to wallow before the wind. It was the northwest monsoon, that blew steadily at this time of the year the whole length of the gulf. There would be no turning back now, Jared thought; he would never see his home in Judah again.

He was amazed to see no signs of fear on the faces of either officers or crew. The big helmsman looked actually happy, though his arm muscles bulged with the effort of holding the steering gear, and his bare chest shone with sweat as if anointed with oil. He saw where Jared stood clutching the rail and called to him sharply, "Ho there, boy —you who stand so comfortably idle—bring me a sup of water from the jar by the mast."

Jared reluctantly let go his mooring and slid to the water jar. He dipped and filled a bowl that was wedged beside it and inched his way back towards the helmsman's high platform. His legs were unsteady as those of an infant just learning to walk. As he was about to hold the bowl to the helmsman's lips a wave caught the ship; Jared spilled the drinking water on the deck. The helmsman's gray eyes, cold as the sea in the rain, regarded him sternly. "Surely it is no sailor that has so uncertain a step. Has he never set foot on a deck before?"

"Indeed never."

"The first rule he must learn is obedience—quick and unquestioning. There is no place on a ship for one who falters in his work. Were my hands not otherwise engaged, you would get a good cuff for your clumsiness."

"But—" Jared said.

"*Unquestioning* obedience!" the helmsman snapped. "Fetch another bowlful, and if you but spill so much as a drop, I will hand over this helm to another and give you a lesson in seamanship that you will not soon forget!"

Jared staggered off. The motion of the ship was beginning to turn his stomach; the deck danced before his eyes; he wanted nothing so much as to lie down in the cool shadow of the sail. He panted for a drink himself, but he dared not delay to take one. He filled the bowl and returned with it, walking as if on eggs. A few drops spilled but the helmsman's eyes were on the far horizon, and he did not notice. He drained the bowl, thanked Jared curtly, and said, "Now go to the shipmaster and ask what else there is for you to do. Perhaps he has overlooked you because you are so small."

Jared turned an angry red. The helmsman laughed. "No, now," he said, "we were all small once." It was the first

sign he had given of being human. He had a stern voice and
a tough manner, this Tyrian, but there was something about
him that made Jared crave his admiration. So he tried his
utmost to walk straight and steady across the deck to the
platform on the prow where the shipmaster was now standing. Jared's stiffness only made him stagger the more ridicu-
lously; one would have thought he had taken too much wine.
No other members of the crew had this trouble; they seemed
all as much at ease as Jared himself was on his native hills.
He tried to look upon the waves as hills—hills of green
water. The trouble was that these hills jumped. And the
ship and Jared's belly jumped with them.

Merbal sent him to fetch a basket of the fruits that was
stowed in the hold to keep it from the rays of the sun. Below
decks the rowers sat, close packed on benches, tugging at
long oaken oars. Yshmael, their foreman, a hard-eyed, sallow-
faced man of Zidon, barked out the rhythm of the rowing.
The oarsmen swung back and forth, back and forth, sometimes joining in the chant. A few of them were youngsters,
not more than two or three years older than Jared, but they
were husky fellows with muscular shoulders and backs. Jared
looked at his arms, lean and stringy as bean-pods, in spite
of his hard work at the mines. He would never be able to
pull at an oar beside the others. He hoped he wouldn't have
to try, for the air down here was close and fetid with the
smell of sweat; the timbers of the ship groaned, and the oars
screeched alarmingly in their square holes.

Jared fetched figs and pomegranates, and rushed for the
open air, holding his hand over his mouth. He would never
have believed that the sight of food could be so disgusting.
He hardly had time to rush to the side of the ship before he
gave up his morning meal. Green and weak, he sank to the

deck beside his basket of fruit. The helmsman was watching him; he was grinning. Jared saw nothing funny about his illness. "I—I have been poisoned," he moaned.

The helmsman's grin turned to a frown. "A touch of the sea and you become a wailing babe," he said. "Get to your feet and take the master his refreshment!"

Jared lurched off. The shipmaster sent him on another errand. And so it went, the whole long day. Between each command, he leaned over the side and gave up more, till there was nothing left in his stomach to give, and still his sickness grew on him, and the bitter taste in his mouth. Yet there was not a moment of rest for him till nightfall.

The monsoon blew steadily; the shipmen wrapped themselves in cloaks and lay down on the deck to sleep—all except the lookout, the man with the lead line at the prow, and the helmsman, not the gray-haired one now but a homely middle-aged Hebrew called Michael. The rowers had stopped rowing, and as many as could find places on deck came there to sleep too. There were so many bodies lying prone, side by side and end to end, that there was no space for walking between. Jared lay against the bulwark, rolling back and forth like a sack of meal. The deck was hard, and after the months at the mining camp, there was little flesh left to cushion his limbs. He pulled himself up to lean on the rail and stare across the black water. His stomach was no longer rising to his mouth, but he was hollow, dizzy, and weak. He had eaten nothing all day. His knees shook so that he could not have stood without support; he clung to the rail and hiccupped feebly.

All around him there was endless space, nothingness. The jagged mountain coastline had been swallowed by darkness; the other ships of the fleet had vanished. There was no light

anywhere but the stars in the black sky. With the setting of
the sun, it had grown cold; the wind whistled and wailed in
the rigging. Shem had been right, more right than he knew;
only the foolhardy embarked on a venture such as this.
Maybe the galley *Mekada* had already passed beyond all
known land. If those who did return from the sea ever told
what it was truly like, surely no one would ever go upon a
ship again.

"My small brother does not like the sea," said a voice.
Wrapped in a cloak, bulking bigger than ever in the light
of the stars, was the gray-haired helmsman. Jared answered
only with a hiccup.

A hand grasped his shoulder, so hard that it hurt. Jared
struggled with tears, and put his face down lest they show,
even in the darkness.

"I too felt so, when I was my brother's size," the voice
went on, no longer harsh and stern as it had been during
the day.

Astonishment made Jared answer. "Surely you were never
so puny as I!"

"Truly I was, on my first voyage. And the sickness of the
sea—I had it too. It will pass."

Jared gulped, only half believing.

"Look—" the man's arm swept in an arc across the glittering sky. "See how much room there is in which to grow, how
much good salt air to breathe."

Jared took a deep breath, and found that he did feel
better.

"My name is Eben," the helmsman said. "My father was
a man of Tyre, and so am I. My mother was a Hebrew of the
tribe of Asher. What does my young friend call himself?"

"Jared, son of Abiel and the widow Mara, of the tribe of

Judah." He stammered, for his teeth were chattering in the night wind.

Eben took the cloak in which he was wrapped and put the folds of warm rough wool round Jared's shoulders.

"But you will need your cloak," Jared protested.

"I have no need of it till I sleep. And I do not expect to sleep this night; the Gulf is a treacherous place, full of reefs and rocks. Michael is a good helmsman but he does not know these waters. I must keep watch by his side till dawn. May you slumber in peace."

"May the Lord watch over me," Jared murmured, curling up in the helmsman's warm cloak, too tired to care any longer what dangers that treacherous sea had in store for him. May the Lord watch over my mother Mara and my brother Shem in faraway Judah, he thought. A tear dropped on the helmsman's cloak. Jared brushed it off hastily.

CHAPTER FIVE

The Great Wide Sea

JARED dreamed of home. Even in his sleep he remembered that the season was summer; sheepshearing was long over; the new lambs had been weaned and the spring grass nibbled down to the roots. It was time to take the flocks to feed beside the streams. Navi, their leader, was loudly voicing his orders to move on to the richer pasturage. Jared wished Navi would not be in such haste; he himself was so comfortable where he lay under the olive tree. Then, for no good reason, Navi kicked him. The breeze of morning blew cold on his bare limbs.

The cloak in which he lay wrapped had been jerked away. Jared came awake of a sudden, and for a moment could not understand why, instead of the familiar hills, his sleepy eyes beheld red mountains that seesawed up and down.

"Lazy one!" cried a stern voice. "Do you not know the sun has risen? Quick—Merbal the shipmaster wishes his morning meal!"

Jared did not wait to find out whether Eben's face was ruddy with the dawn or with anger. He scrambled to his feet and ran to where his nose told him new cakes of meal had been laid to bake in the ashes of a brazier amidships.

He thought himself very hungry, but by the time Bela, the Edomite cook, had loaded him down with fresh hot cakes and a bowl of sour milk, Jared's stomach had turned over again. He was not yet cured of his sickness.

The shipmaster stood beside the helmsman, his bowlegs spread wide, arms clasped behind him, swaying with the motion of his ship as if it and he were made on one piece. He took the food which Jared brought, and for a moment his eyes left the horizon. Yesterday, during Jared's fetching and carrying, the shipmaster had paid him no more attention than if he had been a drop of seawater, but today the fierce eyes, under the bushy, silver-sprinkled brows, examined him with a look of irritation. "So," Merbal said, "it is the young Hebrew who made so much ado about freedom. Yet there seems to be a green pallor on his face—perhaps this freedom does not give him so easy a life as he expected?"

Jared bowed, and said he liked his freedom well enough.

"Had not the King commanded it, I should never have taken aboard one too dwarfish to do his turn at the oars," Merbal said to the helmsman. "This is no training ship for weaklings."

"The boy will learn to make himself useful," Eben said quietly.

Merbal broke a cake of bread, dipped it in the milk, and crunched it in his powerful jaws while he looked back intently over the high stern. The other galleys were still following like a fleet of ducks on a pond. The purple sails were smoothly rounded as if blown of glass; the prow of each ship, curved and sharp as a knife, cut through the blue water; foam streamed from the edges of the wound. But the shipmaster did not seem pleased by the pretty sight. "Do not stand there with gaping mouth, boy!" Merbal barked at

Jared. "Get below and tell Yshmael, the foreman, to quicken the pace. Are we a Nile River barge that we cannot show those other fellows a clean pair of heels?"

Today it smelled even more foul below than yesterday; some of the young oarsmen had been overtaken by a touch of seasickness too. Only the older ones pulled heartily. The flickering sunlight that came through the oar holes dappled the muscular backs glistening with sweat. The foreman nodded grimly at Jared's message and barked out his chant in faster time: "Pull—ho! Pull—ho!"

But when Jared reached the deck again, he saw that in spite of the stepped-up pace, the galley directly astern was slowly drawing abreast of the *Mekada*.

Merbal pointed to it furiously. "Look, look!" he said to the helmsman. "What would the dock loungers of Tyre say now if they saw Merbal's ship a sluggard? Where is your vaunted skill as a helmsman, Eben? Am I to be shamed because you are careless?"

Eben shrugged. "Beliazar's ship has picked up a stray breeze which we, standing closer to the shore, do not feel," he said calmly. "I did not know that Merbal wished to race with Beliazar. I had thought that no unnecessary strain should be put on either the men or the ship at the start of a long voyage."

"The helmsman will keep a civil tongue in his head!" Merbal said. He consulted the manual of sailing directions, clay tablets covered with writing and figures, which lay by Eben's side. "We shall be passing out from the Gulf to the sea within the hour. See that you steer a smart course close to the shore. I know a trick worth more in time-saving than a stray breeze."

He walked forward. A shipman clung to the prow, swinging the line on the end of which was a lead weight for measuring the water depth. Eben gave the helm to Michael for a moment and ran to the side of the ship. Leaning out, he watched the foam thrown up by the prow. "We are approaching fast," he muttered to himself. "Too fast, for the tide begins to pull us toward shore. Merbal risks much for the sake of speed." Seeing that Jared stared and listened, he cried, "Get below on the instant, boy, and tell the rowers they shall be ready to double their efforts. And do you remain close by the deck entrance to relay my orders to them."

Jared clung halfway up the ladder where he could hear Eben's voice above the crash of the seas. His eyes were on a level with the rail, and when the gallery heeled over he could see how it was swinging closer and closer to a rocky headland against which huge white combers were breaking. Eben and Michael both were leaning hard on the steering oars but *Mekada* seemed unwilling to obey them. The wind was cut off by the headland; the sail fluttered and hung limp. The waves were pushing the galley towards the rocks, and a current too was sucking it in. "Tell the oarsmen only they can save the ship from destruction!" Eben shouted to Jared.

The galley was taking the waves broadside now; it would not answer to the helm. It lay so far over that one bank of oars was out of water and useless.

"More speed below!" Eben shouted.

"More speed below!" Jared yelled down the hatch. The sea was roaring in his ears like the Jordan River in flood. A drift of salt spray lashed across his face. He ducked, loosing his grip on the ladder. He caught hold of a rung, barely saving himself from being pitched into the boiling waves.

This was the end of the voyage, the end of his life, Jared thought. How soon it had come! Perhaps the shipmaster

knew some way to save the galley. All Jared could see was
the plunging prow, with a man clinging to it, dangling the
useless lead line. Next moment the prow was buried in
foam, and when it rose again, there was no man there.

The sail was whipping out like a flag. Jared covered his
eyes. He heard the beat of feet upon the deck. What good
did it do to run? You couldn't escape this death by running.
But the motion of the ship eased. Jared opened his eyes and
saw that Kalab and another were hauling on the slapping
sail lines. The sail filled again, round and smooth as a fat
belly. The ship stood up and slowly drew away from the
shore; a puff of wind had reached it just in time. Now the
oars too could bite the water, and the distance between galley
and rocks widened. Slowly the *Mekada* crept past the headland; the lines were slacked off and the ship began to wallow
again, gently, with the steady monsoon behind it.

Jared pointed to the prow and cried to Eben, "There was a
man—the sea took him."

The helmsman's mouth was bitter; his eyes were angry.
"It was Strato, a man of Tyre, and my friend. The sea will
claim many of us before this voyage is done."

The shipmaster showed no sign of strain from the narrow
escape, nor of regret at the drowning, for which he was
surely responsible. Instead he rubbed his hands as he gazed
at the creaming wake behind them and saw that none of the
other ships had yet rounded the headland. "That was the
way to give them the slip," he said. "None of the other masters will have the courage to do as Merbal did."

Eben, silent, gripped the steering oars as if he were
throttling them.

And now the long passage of the Red Sea itself was begun.
The sun shone hot and yellow; the wind sang cheerfully in

the rigging, and the crests of the waves were a lacework of sparkling white. But Jared knew these waves fed on human flesh. Already on this voyage they had swallowed one man and were just waiting their chance to gobble another. To Jared's seasickness was now added the sick weakness of fear. No, the waves were nothing like hills. The hills of Judah were unchanging; they closed in the valleys like comforting guardians. There was never this vast, frightening expanse where wave after wave surged towards the sky, towards nothingness. The shipmen said that over on the right hand lay Egypt, but how did they know? They could not see it.

At sundown, when the oarsmen came up for a rest, they were grumbling loudly. There was no room for proper sleep on this crowded ship; why didn't Merbal put into shore at nightfall, like every other shipmaster, for rest, fresh food, and water? He had left the rest of the navy far behind already.

"I don't like it," said Bela, the cook. His round brown face, though it was half buried in brown beard, had the look of a frightened child. "It's safer for ships to stick together in case of trouble."

Eben told him to be still. "On this ship Merbal is master. His crew may not question his judgments."

For all that second night, *Mekada* sailed before the wind. Jared, tucked in a corner, listened to the talk around him. The shipmen were all, even the Hebrews, experienced sailors. Eli, a young man of the tribe of Manasseh, had gone with Solomon's first ships out through the great stone pillars of the Mediterranean to the Western Ocean. "It would not have surprised me that time never to see Joppa Harbor again," Eli said. "But still I had less doubts than upon this voyage."

"Is there something specially strange about the voyage?"

Jared ventured to ask. Everything about it seemed strange
to him, but he had been comforting himself with the thought
that this was because he was so new to voyaging. "Men have
gone this way before, haven't they?"

"To the Land of Sheba? Often, indeed," said Michael.
There was a puzzled frown on his face, so gnarled and
weather-beaten that it resembled a piece of driftwood. "The
shipmaster—I don't understand him. Why did he take such a
risk this morning? Our poor comrade was lost, and we might
all have been. It was not for lack of knowledge, for Merbal
is well spoken of in Joppa. Why is he in such a hurry? Kalab,
you and Yshmael have sailed with Merbal before; what do
you say?"

"Of course he is in a hurry. He wishes to get the pick of the
Eastern spice markets before the other ships reach them,"
Kalab said. "Merbal drives his ships and his men hard; he is
no master for cowards or weaklings. But he brings back
from his voyages more treasure and trade goods than any
other commander."

"Then Merbal is the shipmaster for me," said Peleg, a
Hebrew of Joppa.

"Well, no one can call me a coward or a weakling," said
Eli, who was freckled, good-natured, and a bit given to
boasting. "This couldn't be a more fearsome voyage than the
time we went to the land where the savages had three heads
and six arms. If our ship hadn't been pointed toward the sea,
so we could push off with speed, they would have slaughtered
us all."

"You actually *saw* such monsters?" asked Ira, a quiet and
serious young man of Dan.

"Who waits to see them?" Eli answered. "When we heard

them crashing through the brush, that was enough. Besides, it was too dark to see clearly."

It was too dark now to see Eli's face; Jared couldn't make out whether to believe him or not.

"This shipmaster—will he take us farther than we bargained for?" Bela asked. "Suppose he doesn't find the gold we're sent for in Sheba? Suppose he decides to look elsewhere for it?"

"Suppose!" said Kalab. "What of it?"

"They say that near the edge of the world, the sun at twilight hisses into the ocean like an ember plunged into a waterpot," said Eli.

Jared felt his flesh crawl.

"Perhaps we'll go through the channel of the Clashing Rocks," Eli said. "There the mountains rise and fall like a butter churn, and no ship can live in the seas they raise."

Jared shivered. "If there's so much to be feared, why do you go to sea?" he asked the young sailor.

"I don't know," Eli said. "Whenever I have been in my village for a while, a longing comes over me to leave it behind again and see the rest of the world." He turned to Michael. "How about you, old-timer? You too are of the tribe of Manasseh. Is it because we live by the coast that the sea calls to us?"

"I thought it had done with calling to me," Michael said. "My old bones have had enough of the cold and damp. But then along came King Solomon's officers, and said the King needed men of experience—and so here I am again."

"It takes courage, young one," Ira said to Jared. "How much courage you will soon see."

"And so you all tell tales to frighten an inexperienced youth!" said Eben's voice out of the darkness.

"They are tales told to us by the Zidonians," Ira said, and Eli added, "Can you deny that in Sheba the frankincense trees are guarded by winged serpents?"

"I can deny it," Eben said impatiently, turning to stand moodily by the rail, staring into the night.

Merbal, wrapped in his cloak, had come among them unseen. "Curiosity reaps its reward in punishment," he said. "Precious things must be well guarded." Noticing Jared, he added, "This is a word particularly to *you*, freedom lover. Don't go rummaging among the stores for anything other than what you have been sent for, or the reward will be a beating."

Jared shrank away, trying to make himself unseen. As far as he knew, he had carried out all Merbal's orders. This Zidonian was indeed a hard master. He was glad when Merbal left the storytellers and returned to the prow, where cushions had been laid down to make him a resting place.

"Eben is in ill humor," Bela whispered.

"It is because of Strato that was washed overboard," Ira said.

It was a clear and moonless night; the sky was thick dusted with stars. Jared stared up at them, thinking of the drowned man, the clashing rocks, the savages with three heads, the shipmaster's harshness. What terrors had he laid up for himself when he had foolishly left his mother and his brother and his home to seek a fortune in Jerusalem? There was no sound now but the lonely sighing of the wind, the swish of the waters along the ship's side. This ship was but a tiny speck upon the vast ocean, and how much smaller was he!

To allay his homesickness, he began to say over to himself silently a psalm of King David's:

How manifold are thy works, O Lord.
In wisdom hast Thou made them all;
The earth is full of thy creatures.

The next lines were no comfort at all, however:

Yonder sea, great and wide,
Therein are creeping things innumerable,
Living creatures, both small and great.

Jared's hand went to his girdle, to the shepherd's pipe
that was hidden there. He had always been able to soothe
himself with a tune. Not thinking what he did or where he
was, he pulled out the pipe and blew upon it softly. As he
played, he improvised, trying to call to mind the sunlit pas-
tures of home, the baa-ing of the sheep, the soft spring wind
that was not to be feared, the streams that purled and sang,
but did not roar like the cruel sea.

He closed his eyes, better to see the familiar things as well
as hear them. So he did not notice how all around him,
sleepers stirred and others came from other parts of the ship
to listen. When he looked up, he found himself surrounded
by a circle of white faces and eyes staring out of the darkness. He heard a sniff. Bela, close by, was wiping his nose
with his fist. Hastily Jared hid the pipe again in his girdle.

They begged him for another song. Jared shook his head,
saying he could not. And after a while when they knew he
meant it, the sailors one by one lay down again to sleep. And
still Jared was restless. He rose and picked his way among
the sleepers to the side of the ship.

There were stars in the sea, as well as above. Where the
ship cut through the water, small cold blue lights danced,
and a whole milky way of them streamed out behind. Jared,

puzzled, stood there and stared. How could there be light without fire, and how could there be fire in the water?

A dozen questions buzzed in his busy brain. He knew of no man on the ship who might answer them but Eben. Yet all this day the helmsman had shown him no sign of friendliness. He was sitting by the steering oars again now; Jared could see his broad shoulders against the sky. He walked up on the poop platform and asked if he might watch by Eben's side for a while.

The helmsman nodded without answering. In the starlight, his face did indeed look grim. So Jared was startled to hear him say in a grave, gentle voice, "My small brother makes music that does the heart good." Then again he was silent. The sea was smooth tonight, and the wind mild and warm; the big poop oars creaking in their sockets, seemed to swing very little.

"Surely the ship does not find its own way by night," Jared said. "Yet how can you steer in the darkness? Or do you have eyes to pierce the night and find the shore, as my eyes cannot?"

"By night there are the stars to steer by," the helmsman said. "See where I point—seven stars in the shape of a plough? If your eyes will make a line from the two that form the handle, they will come to another star. It is Osh, the Northern Star."

"It is behind us," Jared said. "Is it always there?"

"It is always in the north, above the axle on which Arets, the earth, turns like a wheel each night. When we go south, as tonight, we make sure that Osh is behind us."

"How do you know all this?" Jared asked, awed.

"Why, the men of Tyre have been sailing the seas these many years; they have noted down what they learned for the use of others. It is all written on these tablets and charts by my side."

Jared looked up at the sky and again a shudder ran through him. The arch of heaven was so huge and the stars so many. They were a dust of silver scattered over a vast dark mantle. "And what of the stars in the sea?" he said, pointing to the ship's glimmering wake.

"Those are not stars, but small sea creatures disturbed by the ship's passing," Eben said.

"There are also large creatures, terrible monsters, in the sea," Jared said.

Eben shrugged. "The leviathan is big, but he is nothing like so fierce as they say. The Zidonians tell many false tales to frighten others away from the lands where they trade."

"Then there's nothing to be afraid of on the sea?" Jared said hopefully.

"There's plenty to be afraid of, without calling on monsters, clashing rocks, or the rest of that nonsense. There is also, if they can face the dangers, a rich reward for those that sail the seas."

"Gold?" Jared asked.

"Gold perhaps," Eben did not sound interested. "The reward is one thing for one man, another for another. What it is to be for my small brother, and whether it is worth the hardship and danger, he will have to find out for himself."

CHAPTER SIX

Jared's Trials and Temptation

THE next morning, the complaints of the crew were louder. No one had rested well. The two score men or more that made up the crew could not find room to stretch out, even close-packed, on the deck. Many were forced to lie below, in the heat and stench between the rowing benches. There were complaints about the food as well; most of it had spoiled in the heat.

"No man's cookery could cure the meat!" Bela said. "The smell of it is so rank that the flies have come many miles out from the land to hunt it down."

The flies were like a plague from Egypt, stinging and drawing blood. In spite of sweat rolling down, the men wrapped themselves in cloaks to the eyes for protection from the flies and from the fine mist of sand which the scorching wind off the desert had brought with it. Under a sullen sun, the ship sailed like a barge of the dead, crewed by spirits draped in long white garments.

All day Jared fetched and carried, scratching and slapping at swarming insects as he went. He brought meals and messages from one end of the ship to the other. He crawled on his knees, sicker than when he was upright, to scrub down the oaken planks. When this was done, Eben tossed him a scrap of soft linen and told him to wipe the white brine from the rails of polished Semir firwood. It seemed that a ship had to be cared for more tenderly than the house of a rich man.

Eben sent him below for a piece of fruit to quench his thirst, but every morsel Jared could find was soft and rotten. He tossed baskets and boxes aside, hoping to find at least one unspoiled pomegranate or bunch of grapes. Suddenly Merbal was at his back, jerking him upright. "Why are you burrowing like a rat? What are you trying to snuff out?"

"Nothing, nothing but refreshment for the helmsman," Jared said.

Merbal cuffed him and hissed in his ear, "Is it the gifts for Queen Bilkis that you are hunting? They are well hidden. And do not let me catch you babbling of them to the others, or I will have to watch not only you but the whole thieving crew!"

In the early afternoon, a new wind boiled up from the south, hot and wet as steam from a kettle. In a few minutes the rough high chop was tossing the galley about like a straw. The shipmen struggled to furl a sail which only pushed the ship backward. But when it was done even the oars made little headway.

"Can we do no better than this?" Merbal growled in Eben's ear.

"The wind and the current are against us and the men are tired," Eben said. "A night's rest ashore will make for better speed in the morning."

Merbal, frowning, agreed. Jared noticed that the shipmaster respected Eben's judgment in navigation, though they did not seem to be friends. "Turn the ship toward the Arabian coast," Merbal said. "And you, Abu, take your place at the

masthead. Look sharp, now; these coral shores have a bite
as wicked as a wolf's."

Seeing how Abu swayed with the mast, back and forth,
back and forth, Jared prayed that this was something else he
would never be called to do. Abu motioned and pointed, now
to the right, now to the left. Eben, leaning on his oars, followed the lookout's signals.

Jared, free from duties for the moment, leaned over the
rail to see why Abu seemed to be looking down, not out
toward the shore they were approaching. He gave a yelp of
fear.

"What are we afraid of now?" Eben said drily. "Monsters
and sea serpents?"

"Stop—stop—halt the ship!" Jared cried. Too excited to
think twice, he ran to the helm and put his hands on one of
the big poop oars which Eben held lightly under his arm so
that he could quickly change its direction at will. When
Jared grabbed it, the oar swung over wildly. Eben jerked it
back and dealt the boy such a blow that he went down in a
heap. Abu, from the masthead, loudly cursed at the helmsman, and Merbal came roaring from the prow where he had
been directing Peleg at the sounding line.

"Since when do you play games with coral reefs, helmsman? Must I take the helm from you and steer the ship
myself?" His glance fell on Jared, crouching by. "Or was this
monkey up to his tricks?"

Before Jared could answer, Eben said quickly, "I spied a
spur of rock, and made a sudden swing to avoid it; that is all
that happened."

Merbal, muttering, stumped back to the prow. When he
was out of earshot, Eben said, with ice in his voice, "Do
you know how much you put the ship in danger? Reefs and

rocks are thick around us. If we wander so much as an arm's length from the path chosen by the lookout, we may crack upon a hidden ledge. What was the meaning of your sudden madness?"

"May the helmsman pardon one who is so stupid," Jared said, the water standing in his eyes from shame as much as pain. "I thought I saw a whole mountain range of sunken peaks—only a few handbreadths below us. I thought no one saw them but I."

"Our young seaman is beginning to think he knows too much," Eben said, while his eyes still watched the lookout's signals. "No member of the crew may dispute the judgment of shipmaster and the helmsman, not even those far more experienced than you. If Merbal had guessed what you did, he would have killed you. I do not care for killings; that is why I protected you. But the blow I gave you was small punishment for what you did."

"Your servant is grateful," Jared said humbly.

Eben swung the helm over, skirting a patch of broken water where the sea chafed against a coral head, and, unexpectedly, laughed. His teeth were very white in his bronzed face, and his laugh as hearty as a boy's. "So you think I can halt the ship as if she were a mule in harness?"

The bruise on his cheek remained, but the bruise of unhappy shame in Jared's breast began to melt away. He so very much wanted to please the big Tyrian. "I forget the ship is not a live creature. It answers to your will as if it understood you."

"A proper feeling to have for a ship," Eben said, moving his oars ever so delicately in response to Abu's signals. "That is why we give ships names and speak of them as if they were women. This one is a queen of the seas, mind you—

Mekada, which is another name for Bilkis, Queen of Sheba. Treat a ship like a fine, mettlesome woman, do not abuse her, and with luck she will take you over the world in safety. But you cannot pull her back with the steering oars; if you do, she but goes in circles. To halt a ship, the oarsmen must back water together."

"Why did I think the reefs so close beneath us?" Jared asked. "Were my eyes doing tricks?"

"It's because the water is so crystal clear," Eben answered. "It is hard to read the coral seas correctly till one has traveled among them many moons. Abu knows them well."

But Jared put his trust in the helmsman rather than the lookout. Abu had a mean look; he never stared you straight in the eye. Perhaps this came from the many years in which, as a lookout, he had needed to shift his gaze quickly from spot to spot. Eben was now concentrating intently on Abu's signals. He waved Jared away.

Jared went back to the rail for another look below the moving waves. He saw trees of coral stretching their branches up from the far depths, garlanded with floating green moss, fronds of brown leaf and berry. There were pinnacles and valleys, knolls of carved brain coral, groves of waving purple sea fans. Fishes bright as butterflies fluttered their fins among the watery gardens; and others, slim, swift hunters, darted from the mouths of dark caverns. It was the world of Tannin the Sea Dragon, beautiful but terrifying.

Some of the reefs, slimy with brown weed, were poking their noses above water by now. Merbal stood by the helm, directing Eben to steer for a long ledge of black rock over which a lather of suds alternately poured and withdrew. With spray fountaining on either side, the galley shot through an opening in the reefs. The keel grounded gently upon a sandy beach.

Jared and the others jumped into waist-deep water, carrying a hawser ashore to make fast. The ground rolled beneath him as if he were still on a ship, for his legs still held the ship's motion. A flock of terns darted overhead, scolding with shrill cries. Big blue herons left their stiff-legged fishing in the tide pools at the approach of the shipmen, hunched up their snaky necks, and took off into a sunset sky with a great flapping of wings. On the yellow beach, black crabs scuttled sidewise into their burrows, popping their eyes.

Back from the beach, desert wastes stretched away toward high, wine-red mountains. But a mile or so inland there was an oasis, with a spring of clear water, fields of ripe barley, and an orchard of figs and limes. Merbal ordered the grain and fruit to be gathered, saying the galley would be far out of reach next day before the inland farmers discovered their loss. The crew might sleep ashore if they wished; only Kalab, Abu, and Yshmael were to remain on the galley with him. These were the three whom the shipmaster most favored, naturally, because they had sailed with him before. After Eben and Michael, they were also the most experienced of the shipmen. Except for these three, Merbal kept very much to himself.

Those who remained ashore made an evening meal of the plentiful fruits and soon stretched themselves out with yawns and groans of pleasure at the softness of the sand to lie upon after the ship's bare boards.

But a fresh wave of homesickness came over Jared. For the first time in days the spot on which he lay did not heave and sway beneath him, but was steady, solid, and dry. It might have been the soil of Judah on a night spent sleeping out with his flock. The bleak buttes behind the oasis might, in the darkness, have been taken for the hills of Judah. Overhead the stars wheeled in the black sky, the same stars he knew at home.

This was his chance to leave the ship and the rough, tough shipmen: Eli, who told tales to frighten him; Kalab, who kicked him; and worst of all the shipmaster, whom he was beginning to hate. No matter how he tried, he couldn't please Merbal. The voyage would be a misery to the very end, and even if he survived, his chance of a good report from Merbal was very small. Merbal would tell the King that Jared was no good as a shipman, and he would be sent back to the mines.

There were men on this shore; the cultivated oasis proved it. With their help, sooner or later he would surely find a caravan to take him back to his homeland. And once in his native village, no one would ever make a slave of him again.

Jared rose and crept cautiously between the sleeping men. Eben lay with his cloak pulled across his face to keep out the blowing sand. Jared hesitated for a moment, overcome by the sadness of leaving. Eben had been just, patient, and even kind. If only Eben would go with him! But such an idea was nonsense. Why should Eben leave the ship? Seafaring was his life. And Eben had no reason to hate Merbal.

Jared straightened his back and walked up the beach to the gray wind-swept ridges at the edge of the desert. Wind hissed like a serpent through scanty patches of grass. Lightning flashed on scattered boulders, white as bleached bones. A few drops fell, and Jared licked his lips. He was thirsty, and he had no waterskin to carry with him, or any knowledge of where springs might lie when he had left the oasis behind.

The desert, heavy and dark, lay all around him. The air smelled of suspicion. The nearby foothills were not dotted with villages of friendly folk, speaking his language. If he looked for refuge among the strangers here, how would he be able to tell them he had not taken part in the stealing of their harvest?

Fire zigzagged across the sky, lighting up the wasteland. It was the Lord, speaking from His holy mountain of Sinai. More dreadful than anything else, worse than the dangers of the strange land, was the guilt that filled Jared. If he left the ship's company, he would be breaking his word to the King. He had sworn to remain with the ship to the very end of the voyage. And Eben also would know him to be a deserter. He could not run away. He *would* not do it, no matter what Merbal had in store for him.

An iron hand descended heavily upon him. Jared, startled, looked up to see the helmsman. "I am not running away," Jared said defensively. The crash of thunder drowned his words and the hand gripped harder. When silence came, Jared repeated what he had said. "I was just—thinking of home."

Eben loosened his grip and put his arm around the boy's shoulders instead. "This happens at times. Although," he added, "I have had no home these many years—no father or mother, no wife and children, no younger brother. The ship is all my family."

"I have no father," Jared said. "But my mother Mara is a woman very like the ship of which you spoke, and I have an older brother—he is not like you."

They stood watching till the lightning faded and the thunder died away. "Come," Eben said. "If we get no sleep tonight, it will be a harder day than ever tomorrow."

On the beach, the others had not stirred from their snoring. Jared made a burrow in the sand not far from Eben's side.

CHAPTER SEVEN

Ophir Is Sighted

THE morning dawned breathless, white-veiled again with heat. The ship's horn roused the men where they lay sweating in their sleep. Jared determined to work even harder to prove himself. But it wasn't easy to do for a master he so disliked; he did it for Eben.

Merbal at last was convinced that the galley had left the other ships of the fleet behind. Now he regularly brought the ship to shore for rest and provisioning. More often than not, they traveled by night, when it was cooler for the oarsmen, and beached the boat by day. The breeze of evening generally blew toward the land and the breeze of morning away from it. Sometimes there were small settlements where they landed, or camps of wandering herdsmen from whom, for a few coppers, Merbal bought curds, cheese, and dried goat's meat. The sons of the desert were not unfriendly except when the shipmaster's hard bargaining brought on arguments.

Jared made sure he did not spend any more time in the hold than was necessary for carrying out his errands, and the shipmaster seemed satisfied that the boy had got over any notions he might have had about ferreting out the Queen's casket of gifts. Merbal was busy with his trading and the careful accounts he kept on his clay tablets. He no longer bothered to single Jared out for abuse. Not that he was pleasant or amiable. If he was not hungry when Jared brought him a dish of bread cakes or a bowl of curds, he would as like as not fling them in the boy's face. If, on the other hand, he was kept waiting, he would roar his anger, cuff Jared, or kick him. The shipmaster was an impatient man.

But just the same Jared was beginning to take an interest in the ways of ships. Whenever he was not scrubbing or fetching and carrying, he would sit at Eben's feet and ask questions. He gave to the helmsman the respect and devotion he might have given to his father, or to a more understanding older brother than Shem. The other shipmen treated him well; when Eli told his tall tales now Jared knew—and Eli knew that he knew—that it was partly with tongue in cheek. Only partly, however. None of these shipmen were sure of what terrors lay among the unknown seas.

Jared adopted a salty rolling walk that aped the older shipmen and was beginning to talk as if he knew his way around a ship. But it was all in his head; he had actually never pulled on a line or touched an oar. One day when he was flipping a cloth lightly and carelessly along the brine-covered rail, Eben called to him. "Since you know so much, it's time you became something more than a cabin boy. Up the mast with you to the lookout station. And no nonsense about it," he said, at Jared's expression of unbelief.

It was late summer by now, in the month of Elul. Eben had said they were coasting along the shores of Sheba. The ship was well out in mid-channel. It was windless; the sail was looped up to the yard and only the oars stirred any

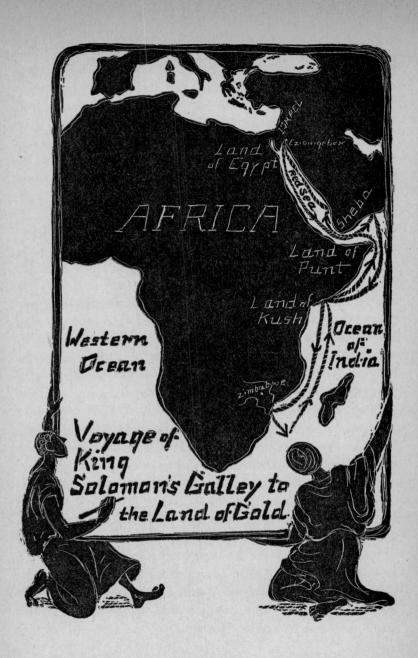

flecks of foam from the flat blue water. Merbal had spoken of the danger of coral reefs inshore, but since there could be none so far out as this, he had not posted a lookout. Jared leaped at the chance to show his mettle.

Because of the calm, the ship was steady and the mast rocked only a little as Jared began to climb it. Of course he had climbed trees at home, but they had been olive trees, low and twisted, with plenty of knots and branches for footholds. The mast was a tall cedar of Lebanon, carefully trimmed of every twig, and smoothed to a fine polish. Jared reached above his head, gripped with knees and bare toes, as he had seen the other lookouts do. He pulled himself up a few arm's lengths, and thought it was not so hard after all. Then he began to slip, and there was no stopping. He slid all the way that he had come, burning the skin from his hands as he did so.

He looked quickly at Eben, and then, with raw hands and knees that soon were skinned and bleeding too, began his struggle again. At last he was able to throw a leg over the yard, pull himself up, and straddle it.

Now he looked down, and that was worse than the climbing. The distance from his perch to the deck seemed much bigger than it had seemed when, from below, he had glanced up at some other lookout. He saw Merbal near the prow, figuring away at some tablets; Eben at the stern, leaning on the poop oar and staring up at him. "Do not look at me; look at the sea!" Eben shouted.

That was what Jared had been trying to avoid. It would make him more dizzy than before. If he fell from this height, he would smash on the deck and break every bone in his body. If he fell into the sea, he would sink like a stone cast into a well. He had never learned to propel himself through

the water like a fish, as some of the younger sailors did
when they sported upon the beaches. The mast swung in
an arc against the sky and Jared swung with it, hollow-
stomached and giddy. He wished now he were down in the
noisome hold. Even on stormy days, the motion of the ship
below had been the gentle rocking of a cradle compared
with this.

He locked his knees around the yard in a deathlike grip,
and steeled himself to look into the depths beside the ship.
They were glassy clear, green as jade, and full of drifting
shadows.

"What do you see?" Eben shouted.

"Nothing!" Jared shouted back, loud as the voice which
stuck in his throat through fear, would let him. "There's
nothing there at all!"

"And on the horizon?" Eben shouted. "Look sharp, now!"

"Nothing either. The sea goes on forever."

Eben paid no more attention to him. Jared wondered how
long he was going to have to stay here, suspended between
sea and heaven. His arms and legs ached, but he did not
dare relax his hold. A warm puff of air touched his cheek;
the mast swayed in wider circles, and the deck beneath
began to roll. The sea heaved gently in a long slow swell,
like the rise and fall of a sleeper's breast. The sun glittered
on it and blinded him. The sweat trickled down into his
eyes; he dared not lift a hand to wipe it away. It was his
duty to keep watch without blinking, much as he longed
to close his burning eyelids, just for a moment. If the ship
grounded upon a reef, the fault would be his alone. He saw
a huge dark cloud beneath the surface; he cried out, and
then saw that it was not a reef but a giant manta ray,
squirming and weaving with its huge black wings. It sank,

and instead, a leopard spotted shark circled the ship, waiting
for Jared to drop into its jaws. All the tales about the horrors
of the deep were true. Jared shuddered and lifted his eyes
to the horizon.

Was it clouds or land he saw at the edge of the sea? He
must not make a fool of himself by crying out again over a
vision that was false. But now he saw columns of smoke
which could only mean the homes of men. Red flecks of
sailing craft dipped and disappeared in a tangle of islands.
Mountains rose, pale blue, and very far away behind a
long low shore of swelling sand dunes.

"Land!" Jared yelled. "Land to the left of us, many furlongs off!"

Eben shaded his eyes and stared for a long moment. He
motioned Jared to come down. When the boy wobbled to
the poop deck, he said crisply, "Well done, lookout. Now go
tell the shipmaster that we have sighted Sheba. I wait his
instructions to turn our course thither."

"So it was you that cried 'land,' poking your nose where
you had no business!" Merbal said. He stumped back to the
poop deck. "I ordered no lookout," he said to Eben. "Who
sent the boy aloft?"

"I did," said the helmsman.

"Since when does Eben take it upon himself to give the
commands?" Merbal snapped. "Does he think I do not know
where we sail? Does he wish to tell me where to go?"

A flush mounted to Eben's bronzed cheek, and his mouth
tightened in an angry line. However he controlled himself
and merely answered, "Indeed, that is not so. I but thought
it would be good training for the boy to station him at lookout. If he is kept at menial errands, he will never learn to be

a shipman. It was merely by chance that he spied the land of Sheba before the shipmaster himself saw it."

Merbal grunted. "The helmsman's excuses are weak! It is no part of his duty to make a shipman of the young Hebrew slave."

"But I am not a slave!" Jared said. "King Solomon said when he sent me with you that I was to learn to be a sailor."

"Keep your impudent mouth closed!" Merbal snapped and hissed in Jared's ear. "I do not know why the King sent you with me. Sometimes I think it was to spy upon me." He turned back to Eben. "Steer the galley well offshore till morning," he ordered.

Eben scratched his short gray curls in puzzlement. "Offshore till morning? It would be dusk by the time we reached the harbor point, I suppose—too dark to find a safe way in through the reefs."

That night the moon rose huge and orange from the land of Sheba, and on the deck the talk was not of sea monsters, but of Bilkis, the Queen, and her treasures. The moon rose higher and made a pathway of pure gold leading across the water to the foot of the port town. A land breeze brought with it the odor of spices and musk, mingled with the salt air.

Merbal had allowed the men to stop rowing, and the ship drifted dreamily. The oarsmen crowded up on deck, filling every handful of space, and hanging on the rigging. Two climbed the mast and perched on the yard, though all they could see of the land was a black sliver at the end of the moonpath. Many crowded around Eben, asking him questions, for he had visited the port of Sheba before this, when he had served in a Sheban ship.

"The city is a mart of Eastern treasures," he said. "Merchants from India and Cathay bring gauzes for the garments of Kings and jewels to decorate their palaces. Ships of the Queen's navy ply between it and Africa. Camel caravans carrying spices, sweet-scented sandalwood, and the juice of the dragon's blood tree, from which frankincense is made, come from the land of fragrance, to the south. You will find ivory in the market place, too, peacocks and apes—all the things men desire for pleasure."

"And is this Ophir, the land where the gold grows?" Jared asked, remembering Shem's stories.

"Men call it Ophir, but gold does not grow here in plenty," Eben said. "The Queen's palace high in the mountains is a wonder house of gold and precious stones, so they say, but these things come in part at least from her colonies elsewhere. The Queen keeps a tight hand on the gold and spice trade; all ships and caravans must pass through the hands of her tax collectors."

Jared dreamed of gold, yellow as butter, as he sat cramped in a corner, dozing fitfully, with his head on his knees. In the morning the ship had drifted out of sight of land. The crew buzzed with angry questions till Merbal stood upon the poop platform and clapped his hands for silence.

"I have been told that there are those among you who wish to make trouble because I have not allowed them to wallow in the pleasures of Ophir." He paused, looked in every face. The men shuffled their feet and looked away. "The price of merchandise in Sheba is too high," he went on. "In the land of fragrance it is different. Spices and gums grow there by nature, and everything can be obtained for less. We shall make a fine profit, and Solomon will be pleased. There will be rich rewards for all of you—but not if you grumble!"

Peleg cheered. The others joined him, saying their master was a clever man. It seemed a reasonable explanation to Jared too, till he remembered the casket for Queen Bilkis which the King had told Merbal to deliver. Maybe Merbal was not going to deliver it at all. Maybe that was the reason the shipmaster was always ordering him to tell no one of its presence.

Merbal was watching him. "On our return," the shipmaster said, "we shall pay our respects to Queen Bilkis and trade for any goods we have not obtained in the South." He scowled at Jared as if to say, that will teach you not to have evil suspicions.

But it was Merbal who had the suspicions, Jared thought. Fancying that he was a spy for King Solomon! What was there for him to spy on, if Merbal was honest? It could only be a matter of a few weeks till the casket was delivered as promised. Nervously, to show Merbal that he had no interest in his doings, he pulled the flute from his girdle and piped a gay tune.

CHAPTER EIGHT

Jared's Adventures Ashore

AT ITS southern end, the Red Sea poured through a passage so narrow that a raft could have crossed from Arabia to Africa without harm in fair weather. But the Straits of Bab-el-Mandeb made a funnel for a wild wind out of the Indian Ocean which drove against the galley, burying its nose in spume. Green water chased Jared the length of the deck as he ran to deliver messages.

When the passage was made, the wind dropped as suddenly as it had come. The African shore faded off into the mists. On the Arabian side, black volcanic peaks pierced the rain clouds. For some days, partly wind-driven, partly under sail, Merbal followed the coast of Hazarmaveth, land of fragrance.

Jared spied the lofty granite cliff which guarded the port almost as soon as the look-out, for the summit, frosted white with bird lime, was a beacon visible many furlongs away. Sea eagles swooped and screamed above the booming surf at the base of the rock. Closer by, a watery entrance appeared; that which had been a peninsula became an island. A bay opened up, and at the head of it was the town, white cubes piled on white cubes, ringed round with a wall. A path led up to the gate between two towers. Jared could hardly wait to see it. If it was as great a port as the one in Sheba—and there was no reason it should not be—it must be wonderful indeed.

The galley was beached among other craft pulled up at the foot of the town. Merbal, all smiles, said that as soon as the men had unloaded his trade goods and carried them to the market place, they were free to enjoy themselves until sundown next day. Only Eben, Yshmael, and Kalab were to remain by the ship, to guard it and to supervise the loading on board of such things as Merbal should secure in exchange for what he had brought.

Jared, staggering under a sack full of copper ingots, paused at Eben's side and said, "Can you not come ashore to see the town, just for a few hours?"

Eben shook his head, smiling. "I do not care about it, young one; the bazaars do not fill my heart with pleasure. I have seen too many of them. Those who deal in them are not my brothers." He reached into his pouch and put a silver coin in Jared's fist. "It is not your fault that you have no shekels of your own. Go now; buy a few dainties; taste of strange foods. You must enjoy an appetite, after our scant fare."

"I do not want to take alms like a beggar," Jared said.

"You can repay me when we receive our reward at the end of the voyage," Eben said.

"Very well," Jared said slowly. "It is not so much for the dainties that I want it, but to buy a trinket for my mother— some beads or perfume, maybe."

"Beads and perfume for an old lady?" Eben said. "Has she desire for such things?"

"She is not an old lady!" Jared said indignantly. "My

mother's hair has not a single thread of gray; she is at least
as young as you!"

Eben laughed. "Well, then, you must take my remark as
flattery, for it means I think of you as a grown man, who
could not possibly have a young mother."

Jared tucked the silver piece with care into a fold of his
girdle, and lumbered down the ladder to join the porters
following Merbal to the town. When he had set his burden
where the shipmaster directed, he dashed off, eager as a
young hound dog on the hunt, sniffing the scent of dung
fires, spices, and leeks frying in oil. The older shipmen, wiser
in the ways of towns than he, had already disappeared.

What should he buy with his silver coin? The white sunshine on the white streets was blinding. Under awnings
spread from the doorways, Jared saw booths piled with
pomegranates, figs, almonds, dates, limes; pastries and sweetmeats that made his mouth water; golden fried fishes whose
crispness he could almost taste on his tongue. But he did
not want to spend his silver piece all at once. And he did not
know how to ask for what he wanted; he did not hear a
word of the Hebrew or the Phoenician tongue in the babble
around him. He saw yellow-skinned men with slanted eyes;
Nubians, tall and glistening black; tribesmen from the hills
with fierce beards, and knives in their girdles.

Jared found himself wedged between a merchant and his
customer: the merchant was snatching the goods from the
customer's hand because the price offered was too low; the
customer was threatening because the price asked was too
high. Blows rained down on Jared's innocent head. He
ducked out and fell against a porter trudging under a huge
load, who cursed him roundly. A moment later a caravan
came through the narrow street; the camels, jingling their

bells, looked down at him with sneering lips as they crowded him into the refuse-littered gutter.

Jared retreated around the corner and found himself in the spice bazaar, where the musky sweet odor of perfumed oils, incense, and sandalwood was a relief. A merchant beckoned to him, holding out a bundle of myrrh. Seeing that Jared could not understand his words, but looked interested in a purchase, the man held up two coppers. Jared held out his silver piece, and the merchant snatched it from him. "No, no, not all of it!" Jared shrieked, pummeling with his fists. The man laughed and gave him a handful of coppers as change. Jared tucked them and the little bundle of myrrh into his girdle. Mara had sometimes said wistfully that she had not had a sweet-scented bundle of myrrh to carry in her bosom since she had been a maiden. Though outwardly she scoffed at such vanities, Jared knew she would be pleased. At last he spent a couple of pennies on some squares of sugary paste that half glued his jaws together.

Perhaps in the morning he would find a small jewel for Mara which he could still afford to purchase. By now it was evening, and his bare feet burned so from the hot streets that he felt he could not walk another step. Not knowing where to look for shelter, he curled up in a doorway to sleep. The breeze of night set the palm fronds to rattling; their starlit shadows danced on the walls. Behind those walls, in the courtyards, he could hear the pound of dancing heels upon the pavement, the jingle of silver bells on ankle and toe, and the queer whining music of an Eastern flute.

Once during his sleep he thought that Merbal was tugging at his tunic, ordering him to be at work. Bold as a lion in his dreams, Jared told the shipmaster to be off. In the morning he woke cramped, hungry, and thirsty, but eager

to see more of the city. A water seller passed by, calling out
his wares. Jared reached into his girdle for a copper. There
was nothing there. He unwound his loosened girdle and
shook it out. It was quite empty. Jared knelt on the doorstep
where he had slept and hunted in each crack and crevice,
but all he found was dust. Tricky fingers had picked his
wealth from his girdle while he dreamed.

He was desolate. He had no more money, not a penny,
and even his cheap little present for Mara was gone. Here
he was in a town where luxuries were gathered from the
four corners of the earth, and he couldn't buy any part of
them. He would have to do without food for the rest of the
day too. He wrapped his girdle tight around his growling
stomach and set out to find a well or a spring where he could
at least quench his thirst. There was usually one on the
outskirts of a town. He had one thing to be grateful for; he
had left his flute on the ship, so that at least had not been
stolen.

Not wanting to chance a meeting with the shipmaster, he
went out from the town by a different gate than the one by
the harbor side. From this gate also a path led to the beach,
and beside it a fresh-water stream tumbled down from the
distant mountains to the sea. Jared drank and washed himself
before walking along the beach to the landing place. There
was no hurry; it was not yet afternoon.

The salt air smelled good after the town. The brilliant sun
made everything shimmer and sparkle. Even the dry sand,
well above the water, glittered. He knelt to scoop up some
of the pretty stuff, and let the quartz pebbles, big as peas,
and the grains of pink and white sand slide through his
fingers. Why—the pink and white was peppered with gold
dust! He had made a great discovery—a gold mine on the

beach! He would bring a sampling of it to the ship, and all
the shipmen—even Merbal—would acclaim him. But there
was much more common sand than there was gold, and he
had no way to sift out the golden grains. He did not even
have a pouch in which to carry his sample. He took off his
girdle again and knotted it into a makeshift sack. As soon as
he had it full, he found another spot where the gold seemed
to be thicker, so he dumped out all he had gathered and
started fresh. Each sand dune and hollow seemed to promise
more riches than the one before.

He was startled from his treasure hunt by the blast of a
ram's horn. It sounded like the signal horn which his own ship
carried. Could it be that Merbal was leaving ahead of time?
Jared began to pad along the beach, panting under the
weight of his sack and hearing the horn bleat more and more
urgently, like a ram in pain.

When he came in sight of the galley poised where white
beach met rippling green, he could see that it was already
being pushed into the water. Breathless, he shouted, "Wait,
wait!" He pounded along, seeing through blurred eyes that
the galley was now floating. By the time he reached the
landing place, it was already some yards out into the bay.
Merbal had left without him. Merbal had always wanted to
get rid of him. It was no easy life on the ship but it was
better than being left behind.

He could not swim. If he ran out into the water, the waves
would suck him down to his death. But if he didn't, he'd be
stranded in this strange, faraway land. The ship, loaded with
Merbal's purchases in the land of fragrance, must now be
ready to turn back, to head for home. But he, Jared, left
behind, would never find his way home. It was too far; no
ships plied between this place and Ezion-geber. What good

would the discovery of the golden sand do him if he couldn't
bring it home?

He could see the men scurrying about the deck of the
Mekada, making ready to set the sail. He could see Eben at
the stern with his gray hair standing up in the breeze like a
kingfisher's crest. Eben had his hand to his mouth, hallooing,
but the meaning of what he shouted was carried away by the
wind. The helmsman lifted his arm and a rope snaked out
across the water to drop at Jared's toes. Jared grabbed it and
knotted it quickly under his arms. He was jerked from his
feet and dragged over the pebbly shore. And then, as Eben
began to pull in the rope, brine poured into Jared's eyes, his
nose and mouth. Waves closed over his head. He saw green
water above him. A rushing sound filled his ears. He was
torn apart between the pull of the rope and the waves that
dragged him back. He held his breath till he thought his
lungs would burst. He could hold it no longer.

He came to on the deck of the galley. Eli was sitting on
him, pushing on his ribs. Why don't you let me be; haven't
I suffered enough? he thought. But he had no voice with
which to say it; only a croak issued from his blue lips. Eli
pumped up and down; water rushed from Jared's nose and
mouth. His throat was raw; his stomach sick. He heard
Michael say indignantly, "Did the shipmaster have to be in
such a hurry that he could not even wait some minutes for
the boy?"

Another voice—Abu's perhaps—answered, "The shipmaster would have been glad to be rid of the little nuisance."

Eben said, "Nuisance, is it? The boy works as hard as any
full-grown man on this ship!"

"It was not I that called him a nuisance but the shipmaster," said Abu's oily voice.

"*I* like our young brother well enough," Eli said. "He has courage for one so small."

"Not so small as he was at first either," Eben said. "He may yet grow big enough to put fear into those who torment him. Look now—he is beginning to wake."

Jared sat up, gasping and swallowing air as if he were a fish hauled out of the water in a net.

"So the drowned man lives, does he?" Eben said.

Jared blinked, and still thought he could not speak. But when he spied the girdle sack lying limp and flat by his side, he pounced on it with a howl.

"We had to pry this from your fist," Eli said. "What is there about it that is so dear to you?"

"G-gold!" Jared said hoarsely. "It was filled with gold!" He struggled to open the wet knots. He turned the whole thing inside out. All the sand had seeped away except a few damp grains which clung to the folds.

He grabbed Eben's arm. "Turn back—oh, tell the shipmaster that he should turn back! There is a mine of gold on the beach—all the gold that Solomon could possibly wish for!"

Eben glanced at the girdle, picked out some of the gold specks, and flicked them away with a smile of pity. "This is what they call fool's gold—and you are not the first to be fooled by it. If gold were as common as the sands of the beach, it would have no value."

Jared's face changed from blue to scarlet.

"Did Merbal come back with gold from the markets?" Peleg asked Eben.

"Very little, I think, judging by the weight of the chests that were carried aboard. Most of our new cargo is incense and gums and spices."

"But what of the gold we were sent to fetch?" Peleg persisted. His sharp nose and small eyes gave him the look of an eager rat. "The gold of Ophir? Is this not the land of Ophir?"

"It is Ophir, the market place for the gold of far countries. It is not the country of the mines themselves," Eben said.

"Then where are those mines?"

"Some say in the land of Punt. Some say in Kush. Some say further south in Africa than either of those kingdoms. Some say not in Africa at all, but in India. Only the Queen of Sheba and her shipmasters know where the mines are."

"For my part, I don't care," said Bela, the cook. "What I'm interested in is seeing my home and my wife again. We've been at sea for too many moons already. Now that we've a fine cargo below decks, we'll head for Ezion-geber."

"Have I a crew of shipmen, or of old women gossiping at the well?" cried Merbal's harsh voice. "There is a fresh breeze blowing up out of India, and I need all hands to make sail. Lively now; if you grow so sluggish from one night spent ashore in a town, I will not give you such leave again!" He passed Jared by with a frown, with no more attention than if he had been a bit of waste that had been washed overboard, and unfortunately washed back again to clutter up the deck.

The shipmaster pointed out into the purple mists of evening, where the waves rolled away to the sky. "There, where Guardafui, the great eastern horn of Africa, stretches into the ocean of India—that is your steering point, helmsman. See that you do not waver from it, for we must make round it southerly while we can."

The shipmen exchanged glances. Southerly? their eyes questioned. Ezion-geber lay northwest. The course Merbal had given was southeast. If they were not returning home, for what strange land were they headed now?

Jared barely suppressed a moan. He had promised the King to remain with the ship till the end of the voyage, but how long was this voyage to be? Then he shook his damp curls as if he were shaking the brine from his eyes. This longing for home was a sickness. He was determined not to give in to it longer. He was determined to be a shipman, like Eben. And one thing he would do as soon as the chance came: learn so to conduct himself in the water that he would not swallow half the sea if he came into it again.

CHAPTER NINE

The Ship Reaches Punt
After Sore Trouble

ELI said that not even in the Western Ocean had he seen waters so uncertain as those between Arabia and Africa. The air was still as death, but a mysterious current carried the ship before it. Every few hours Jared ran to look over the side; the bits of rubbish Bela had thrown overboard after the morning meal were still in the same spot, keeping the ship company. But once in a while a piece of old planking or a half-rotted oar suddenly appeared in the midst of the familiar items. If these had bubbled up from the depths, might they not also as suddenly be sucked down again, and the ship with them?

For a time the current set toward Africa, and Merbal was pleased. Afterward it reversed itself, and the ship moved slowly backward to where it had been before. Merbal kept the men at the oars, fighting against this tide, but it was too strong for them.

"If we continue like this," Eli said frowning, "we shall drift forever and die of hunger and thirst."

"What do the clay tablets say we should do?" Jared asked the helmsman, hunting for reason to keep up his courage.

Eben did not answer, but Michael said, "We have no sailing directions for the Ocean of India."

And Eli added, "Nor has anyone on the ship ever been this way before."

"Not even Eben?" Jared whispered.

"Not Eben, not I, not even the shipmaster."

"Shebans come this way," Eben said, "but they keep their knowledge to themselves." He looked up at the sky. "If the clouds lift, we will steer by the direction of the sun."

"If we can break loose from the current," Michael reminded him.

"How does the shipmaster dare to go on?" Jared burst out.

"He will dare anything," Bela said gloomily.

At night the sky was a smouldering canopy; no one could sleep. There were no stars, nor any land in sight, but Merbal stationed Peleg on the prow with the sounding line. All night Jared heard the monotonous voice calling out that there was no bottom.

The flat, far edge of the sea stood out against a flash of light. "At last a storm comes to clear the air," Michael said.

But it was not a storm; there was no thunder. "Look—look, it comes straight for us!" cried Bela the cook, his beard quivering with terror. As the streak of fire flew toward the ship, Jared shrank away from the rail, expecting smoke to pour from the wooden planking at the touch of this thing. But instead the glowing band blew out like a lamp. "It is demon fires," Bela moaned.

At dawn a bitter wind came sweeping out of the night desert. The sail, which had been hanging limp, shuddered. Swollen, smoky clouds rolled up from the horizon till the whole sky was a dirty gray. "Get in the sail!" Merbal yelled, but the squall struck so swiftly that the lines had only just been unloosed when they were torn from the men's hands. The sail's shaking made the whole galley shake from end to end. Eben struggled to keep it head-on into the waves. Thunder over Africa echoed the thunder of the flapping sail.

With a loud crack, the sailcloth split from top to bottom. The ship was quite out of control, and would surely have gone over if the rain had not poured out of the sky, flattening the sea. The wind dropped; the squall had passed.

Eben grinned. "That is the kind of fight I like—a clean fight against the elements. None of the bullying and threatening and arguing that men do!"

Jared wondered if he would ever learn to be so unafraid.

There was extra linen in the hold, but no room to stretch out the torn sail and repair it under way, so it was stripped from the yardarm and stored below. Then Bela, spying a new horror, cried out, and crouched down among his cooking pots, covering his eyes.

"What ails you?" Eben called out.

"We have reached the whirlpool of doom," Bela croaked. "We are all to be devoured!"

Jared was afraid to look over the side, but curiosity overcame him, for all around the ship a hissing sound arose, like broth boiling in a giant cauldron. It was a death hunt. Big fish were chasing little fish, which leapt from the water by thousands in their attempt to escape. The water was foul with their half-chewed bodies. And from the midst of this battlefield, like a volcanic island rising from the sea, a shining black monster heaved itself up, belching and rumbling, blowing a stream of white water into the air.

"It is the leviathan," Eben said. "If we do not disturb him, he will do us no harm."

Jared did not believe it. The whale was so big that one flip of its tail could smash in the galley's fragile sides.

The oarsmen, hearing Bela's cry, burst from their benches and swarmed up on deck, staring at the horrid sight. The Phoenicians flung themselves on their knees, taking out amulets and small images of Melkarth and Ashtoreth with whom they pleaded for mercy. Jared too murmured a prayer for protection.

Merbal had been sleeping, wrapped in his cloak on the bow platform. Roused by the shouting and confusion, he came aft in a fury. He had picked up a length of rope, and with it he laid about him, striking men right and left.

"Get below, you dogs!" he bellowed. "Can I never shut an eye without some treachery behind my back?"

"We have reached the end of the world," Bela cried. "We dare not go farther."

"That's right; no farther!" shouted an oarsman defiantly. And the others echoed him, crying out, "We must turn back!"

"Turn back, is it?" growled the shipmaster. His rope lashed out and the man fell groaning. Merbal stood planted, swinging the rope, facing the frightened crew. "And what of the King's orders? If I turn back without bringing Solomon his gold, what will your punishment be? The punishment for those who mutiny against the King's shipmasters makes the fate of those bleeding fishes seem a kind one!"

Bela flung himself down at Merbal's feet and grabbed the hem of his tunic. "Master, master," he cried, "how many more signs must you have that this voyage is cursed? Bewitched tides, demon fires, a sail ripped asunder, and now this horror of devouring! We will never reach the land of gold!"

Merbal kicked Bela away. "Cowards you are, all of you!

When was treasure ever found without hardship and danger? Must you whimper and wail because some upwelling of the tides sets a feast of creatures before you? It is the law of the universe that the strong prey upon the weak, whether they be fish or men!"

The whale had sunk back into the depths. But still the bloated fish corpses floated all around the ship, white bellies upward. Jared shuddered to think that the next time the leviathan emerged, it might be to swallow the ship, and the corpses might well be those of himself and his comrades. The shipmen stood muttering, shifty eyed, afraid to look upon the sea, afraid to meet Merbal's scornful stare. The whipped one had crawled away to hide his pains.

"Come then," said the shipmaster, impatiently. "Let us be men, not jellyfish! Our rewards are almost in sight. The Queen of Sheba has mines in Africa that are rich beyond all belief. These are our goal. If you go willingly, each will get a share of the gains. If not—" He lashed again with his rope. This time the end of it flicked across Jared's legs. It was no more than a bee sting, but it infuriated the boy. "Even as the leviathan is stronger than the little fish," Merbal said, "so am I stronger than you lily-livered scoundrels. And you will do what *I* say!"

Again he stared at his crew, and again they could not meet his eye. "Soon we shall round the cape and go ashore," Merbal went on. "We shall trade our cheap baubles for precious things. And you would turn back now? Speak up; let me see how many of you are men!"

"I will go on!" shouted Kalab.

"And I!"

"And I!"

"And I!" shouted others among the crew.

I'll show him that *I'm* a man, thought Jared. "And I!" he squeaked.

"We can't be put to shame by the youngest amongst us," Michael said. Eli and Ira nodded slowly. The tide was turned.

Only Eben had taken no part in the argument. "Well, helmsman?" Merbal asked. "What do you say in the matter?"

The big Tyrian's face, gaunt with the strain of hours at the helm, was quite expressionless. "The shipmaster knows I but carry out his commands," Eben said.

"My command is to continue south, to the land of gold."

The oarsmen went back to their oars, and Merbal to the bow, but the others lingered on the afterdeck.

"You did not pray when we were in danger," Abu said to Eben. "The gods will punish you."

"I have seen too many gods in too many different lands to believe in the power of any," Eben said. "The Baal of the Phoenicians is a cruel god that asks for the bodies of innocent babes to be consumed upon his altars. Should I pray to such a one?"

Horrified, Jared cried out, "Human sacrifice is an abomination!"

"So *I* think, but the priests of Tyre and Zidon demand it. Even though I should be destroyed for my defiance, I will ask no favors of Melkarth and Ashtoreth. Tell me, Jared, is your god more kind? I was a small child when my Hebrew mother died, so I know nothing of him."

"He is just," Jared said.

"You carry no image of him," Eben said. "I have watched you at your morning prayers."

"Images are forbidden to us," Jared said. "Why should I need an image, when He is everywhere?"

"This is a different sort of god from the ones I know," Eben said thoughtfully.

The squall had done nothing to cool off the weather, though it had cleared the clouds from the sky. The sun was as brazen as the image of Melkarth, the Sun-god, in the great temple at Tyre. Tar bubbled between the planks.

"Oh!" Jared cried, dancing from one foot to the other. "It burns, it burns!" Eben told him to wrap his feet in rags against the scorching deck.

"The heat in the torrid zone can be so great that ships catch fire," Eli said. "Sometimes the sea boils up and thickens, and the ship is caught fast in a jellied sea."

"Be still, Eli!" Eben snapped. "Have we not had enough trouble without your childish tales?"

But far more dangerous to the peace of the ship was Abu, who went about muttering that Melkarth was angry at the helmsman and that was why the sun shone so fiercely. Though the crew were used to its rays, they all suffered in the days that followed. Jared was burned so brown that Eli teased him, saying he could be taken for a man of Kush if it were not for his blue eyes. But the eyes grew red rimmed from the glare; the skin peeled from Jared's snub nose, and his lips were cracked and sore. Eli, who was fair complexioned, was a mass of freckles and an angry pink heat rash; he itched miserably and made himself worse by scratching.

Merbal kept the men at the oars day and night; they dared not rebel against his orders again. They were all thirsty, for drinking water was so scarce that Bela, who was in charge of the water jars, could give only a cupful a day to each man. Some of them muttered against Merbal, and others, prompted by Abu, against Eben.

Jared overheard these remarks, and already made irritable
by the heat, he fidgeted and fumed at his own helplessness.
For he feared that Eben would be blamed if they did not
soon reach land. Eben would laugh at such an idea, so Jared
merely said, "I cannot stand this idleness. Even Merbal asks
nothing of me, and all I can think of is the heat. I am going
to tell Yshmael to let me have a turn at the oars."

Eben viewed him with approval. "Good," he said. "This
is a time when any fresh effort is a help to the ship."

Above decks Jared had been roasted as on a spit; below,
he found the oarsmen baking to death slowly. A dizzying
pattern of flickering ripples was reflected on the ship's sides,
the deck overhead, and the bare, wet, swaying backs. The
men were a crew of skeletons languidly bending and pulling.
They were so weak from heat, work without rest, and scanty
food that Yshmael could not make them step up their pace
no matter how much Merbal threatened. None of them had
spirit left to join in the chant. The extra deck hands had all
been called to help; many of the oars were being handled by
two men. This made the benches even more crowded, the
air more close.

Jared saw Eli rowing glassy-eyed and slipped into the
place next to him. Eli, moving over to make room, gave a
disappointed grunt when he saw it was the small one who
had come to share his burden. Jared's will was good, but he
did not know how to row. "Leave be, if you can't keep in
time," Eli said irritably. "Must you hang on the handle so
that I have your weight to pull as well as everything else?"

"Let me try—I'll catch the way of it soon," Jared panted.
He watched how the rowers pushed forward with straight
arms, how their bodies bent low between their knees, then
the backward pull of arms and shoulders, ending up with

a chorus of grunts. He kept his eyes on Eli and tried to do as he did. After a while he was rewarded by a sickly grin.

"Put your back into it," said Eli hoarsely. "There now, both of us together!" The oar gave a sudden jerk and Jared fell from the bench. Nearby oarsmen laughed, but as he sheepishly climbed into place again, they called out to him, "That's the way, small brother!"

Jared pulled till his hands blistered, his back ached, and his arms seemed made of lead. But he knew he must not stop. Even the little that he did was needed. His head was swimming; he struggled in a daze, thinking after each stroke that he could last for only one more. And one more. And one more again.

The high shrill cry of the lookout sounded overhead. "Land—land!" he was calling. The men stopped rowing; Jared crumpled into a heap. Eli picked him up and carried him to the air. "I'm—I'm well enough—leave me be!" Jared staggered to his feet. Far, far away, above the blue horizon, a cloudy shape floated.

A long sigh came from the shipmen. In a little while, refreshed by their hopes, they brought the galley around a headland and to rest in a sandy lagoon. Merbal said they had reached the Land of Punt.

CHAPTER TEN

Ivory, Apes, and Savages

FOR weeks Merbal traded along the coast wherever a column of smoke, rising above the jungle, showed the presence of man. There were many small sluggish rivers where villages of straw-roofed huts stood on piles in the water. When the galley approached, dusky-skinned men with dark pointed beards and hair cut Egyptian fashion came with their enormously fat wives to see what the strangers had to offer. In these places a definite system of bargaining had been worked out by the traders from Sheba, so that not even language was necessary.

A fire would be made to attract attention, and nearby a collection of trinkets would be spread on the beach: copper bracelets, bead necklaces of Phoenician glass, cloth tinted gayly with Tyrian dyes. Then the galley would pole out into the stream and in a little while the villagers would appear with whatever they thought a fair amount to give in exchange. If it was not enough, Merbal did not touch it till they came again with more. Sometimes he would give a feast as a sign of friendship.

Soon the forward part of the galley was stacked with bundles of herbs, leopard skins, and the ivory tusk of the elephant. Merbal had a right to be pleased, but he grumbled because the natives of Punt had no gold.

"He should have traded for gold in Hazarmaveth or Sheba," Bela said sullenly. "There was plenty to be had in civilized places without going on such a chase as this."

"Ah, but the price was not right," Abu said.

"I'll wager the other shipmasters of the fleet thought it fair enough," Eli said. "How else did King Solomon find gold for his temple? Was it necessary to come to Africa in search of it?"

Jared's favorite cargo was a monkey which, it was said, would bring its weight in silver among the queens of Solomon's Court. The crew named the monkey Methuselah, for he was gray-haired, with white cheeks, a wrinkled face, and bright eyes, like an old man. At first he sat for long periods of time, pulling a grave countenance and scratching his white fur belly as if thinking deep thoughts. But when he became used to the ship, he was seldom quiet. He climbed the mast, swung himself in the rigging by his long curling tail, chattered constantly, and imitated whatever the shipmen did. Jared was Methuselah's special friend and often gave the monkey bits of food from his own bowl. When Jared wiped down the rails or scrubbed the decks, Methuselah would follow behind, doing it too. He was not much of a help, but his tricks made everyone laugh.

Everyone, that is, except the shipmaster. Merbal was angry when the monkey distracted the men at their tasks. The oarsmen could never exert themselves enough to please Merbal. Sometimes he would stand at the stern, looking back as if he still feared to see the other ships of the fleet appear. Only when he was dickering in trade did a smile come to his face.

One evening the galley pulled into a wide marshy river and dropped anchor some yards from the bank where stood a larger settlement than any they had so far visited. A stockade surrounded it; fishing nets were hung up to dry between the peaked-roof huts; behind them fields of grain and root vegetables drove a green wedge into the wild bush country.

"Shall we bring out the goods?" asked Abu.

"Not yet," Merbal said. "This is the land of savages; it is better to wait for a sign of friendliness."

From across the water came the excited babble of voices. A drum began to beat. The shipmen lined up along the rail, watching, till the gate of the stockade opened and a procession marched down to the beach. These men were Nubians, with skins of ebony, and ostrich-plumed headdresses that made them tall as giants. As they marched, they chanted a deep-throated song.

The sound somehow sent a shiver through Jared. It did not seem threatening; but it was quite unlike the gentle, rather sad chants of his own village, or the whining nasal songs of Arabia.

"They carry no weapons," Merbal said. "Take the ship to the shore."

A dozen Nubians, shouting their greeting, ran to pull the galley up, wading into the water and surrounding it with eager cries. The gangway was lowered and the shipmaster stepped down to the beach, followed by his crew.

Within the village, the drums were rolling again. At the gate of the stockade, the chieftain appeared. Jared had never seen any man so like a proud, mighty beast of the jungle. He moved with the grace of a great cat. He was at least seven feet tall and his headdress was so towering that a weaker man could not have carried it. A robe of lion skins flowed from his shoulders; a broad band of beaten gold circled his column-like neck; bangles of gold wire covered his arms from wrist to elbow, and his shins from ankle to knee. Behind him four men carried a pole from which hung the carcass of a big buck.

The chieftain extended his arm in greeting. "Mombambo," he said, pointing to himself, and then spoke some words of welcome in the Sheban tongue. Jared gathered that the meat was a feast offering.

Merbal, who spoke a little of the language, made the proper speech of thanks. Bela bustled about the beach, superintending the digging of a pit and the kindling of the cook fire. Merbal called Jared and said, "Fetch a jar of wine from the ship. Quick; no nonsense now!"

Jared climbed aboard, falling over himself in his hurry. He undid the lashings of a wine jar, but just as he lifted it to his shoulder, a leathery little hand grabbed him by the ankle. He barely managed to recover his balance without dropping and smashing the earthenware jar. "Methuselah!" he cried angrily. "Do you want your best friend to be in trouble?"

Methuselah cowered, with apologies in his beady bright eyes. Jared set down the jar carefully and scratched the ruff of fur about the monkey's neck. The creature ran up his leg to his shoulder and laid his cheek against Jared's. "No, now, little brother," Jared said. "You must learn to behave. This is no time for monkey tricks." Methuselah chirped, but Jared could take no more chances of being tripped up or followed. He put Methuselah below and fastened a hatch cover above him. He did not bother to tie the monkey up, because he was in too much of a hurry. Merbal was always very angry when he was slow in carrying out orders.

There had never been a feast like this one. Bela was at

special pains to show the savages that he could make their meat into a dish more succulent and tasty than any they had known. The carcass of the buck was rubbed with olive oil and herbs. Jared stood by the fire under Bela's direction, turning the roast and basting it till the skin was a crackling brown. Jared's nostrils quivered at the smell of it, and when no one was looking, he pulled off a tiny scrap of skin and popped it into his mouth, burning both fingers and tongue thereby.

The shipmen sat on the seaward side of the fire, and the Nubians on the other, closer to their village. They drooled and licked their lips as they watched the juice dripping from the spitted flesh to the embers, and smelled the rich pungent odor of roasting meat and spicy herbs.

Merbal poured the wine into one of his finest copper bowls and offered it to the chieftain. Mombambo's white teeth gleamed his pleasure at the first taste. The fermented juices brewed by the savage tribes were as muddy river water compared with the red wine of the Judean grape. The bowl went from hand to hand and mouth to mouth, greeted with belches of appreciation. When it reached the side of the fire where the shipmen were sitting, Merbal took it and returned it again to the chief. The shipmen cried out their vexation. "Fools!" Merbal said. "This is no time to grow sodden, thinking only of stomachs. There is work to be done tonight!"

Jared was sent for a second jar of wine, and a third. He marveled at Merbal's hospitality. The shipmaster had never been so generous before. The sight of Mombambo's gold ornaments, Jared thought, must have driven Merbal quite out of his head.

Two of the Nubians began to beat upon their drums; the rest sat cross-legged, swaying their bodies, even more glistening black now from the grease which they had smeared upon themselves while eating. They began to chant again, more and more wildly as the wine was passed around. Some of them got up to dance, shuffling and shaking their shoulders, pushing their stomachs in and out, twisting their faces into wild and horrible grimaces. The dying embers threw leaping shadows against the stockade wall; the drums throbbed, and the chanting was punctuated with sudden ferocious outcries. Around the firelit circle hung the black night of Africa, brooding wilderness on the one hand, lapping water on the other.

Mombambo sat straight and silent, with folded arms.

Merbal was growing impatient. "It is time to trade," he said to the chief.

Mombambo shook his head; stood up, ordered his people to stop their dancing and chanting, and pointed to the shipmen. "Now you make song for me," he said. "Where your drums?"

The shipmen had their chanteys, used to keep time in rowing or heaving on lines, but they had no instruments.

"Let the boy lead us in our singing with his flute," Eben suggested. "This will be as rare a treat to them as the Judean wine."

Merbal ordered Jared to perform. Jared took the pipe from his girdle with a beating heart. The white, rolling eyeballs of the tribesmen were fastened on him. He put the flute to his lips and blew upon it a song he had often heard the shipmen sing as they drew up the sail. At first he was uncertain, but the piping grew in strength as the men joined in with him. The chant had a powerful beat to it, a chorus of shouts at the end of each phrase. The savages sat listening on the other side of the fire. Some of them, overcome by wine, began to doze, their heads drooping. And in the

shadows at the edge of the river, the ship sat as if it too were listening.

At the end of the song, Mombambo bowed deeply, walked to Jared, and put out his hand for the flute. Shocked, Jared stepped back, holding his dear instrument clasped to his breast.

"Give it to him!" Merbal commanded.

And Eben said, "It is an insult if you do not. You must let him have it, small brother."

Jared gave over his pipe as if he were parting with a piece of himself. This flute was the only thing he had left to remind him of home. Many times he had forgotten his loneliness in playing upon it. Mombambo took it from him, bowed again, and ordered one of the skin-covered drums to be presented to Merbal.

"My pipe—my pipe!" Jared cried pitifully.

"Say nothing, boy—our lives may be at stake," Eben whispered. "Inflamed with wine as they are, these savages are quick to anger. Merbal may have cause to wish he had not been so hospitable."

Indeed, Mombambo's eyes were bloodshot, beads of sweat stood upon his brow, and he swayed like a pine tree in the wind. By the light of the red embers he looked enormous, threatening. "Now we trade," he said. Four of his men staggered off to the village and returned with a huge bundle wrapped in leopard skins. It was a treasure of ivory; not the raw tusks but horns and cups and intricately carved images of men and animals. Some had tiny ornaments of gold upon them. The chieftain pointed to the wine jar and held up ten fingers.

"Ten jars of wine for this?" Merbal snorted. "It is too much!"

A second store of ivory was brought.

Mombambo scowled; angry words poured out in his native tongue. Jared thought, the sacrifice of my pipe is going to be useless. If Merbal enrages him with this bargaining, the chief is going to kill us anyway.

"Bring me gold!" Merbal demanded.

"Why you want gold?" Mombambo asked, staring at Merbal curiously. "No gold here. Much gold in the south. From there, these things." He touched his necklace and bangles. "Pretty but not good like the ivory."

"Then let me have your gold ornaments," Merbal said, and impatient, he put his hand on the chief's gold collar.

Mombambo flung him away. Those among Mombambo's warriors who were still awake growled like angry lions at this affront to the person of their chief. Some pulled out knives which they had concealed upon them.

"Get back to the ship, all of you!" Eben shouted to the shipmen, not waiting for Merbal to give the order. Merbal glowered, but fear showed on his face too. They all ran to the galley. Jared, in spite of the warning, hung back for a moment. He wanted his flute. But it was clutched tightly in the chieftain's huge hand; so tightly that the fragile instrument was in grave danger of breaking in two. "Come on, young fool," Eben shouted, grabbing him by the curls.

They pushed the galley into the water and climbed aboard. The Nubians were too drunk to follow. Merbal sent the oarsmen to their posts. "Shall we row out of the river?" Yshmael asked.

"Wait," Merbal said. "We are safe enough here for a time." He ordered several wine jars to be put on the high poop deck close to the gangway, where the savages on shore could easily see them. "Gluttony will make the chieftain change his mind," Merbal said.

And so it was. The warriors—those who could still stand— gathered round Mombambo, arguing loudly. One lifted a discarded wine jar to his lips, and smashed it angrily against a rock when he found not even a drop remained. Others pointed to the ship, to the wine jars on the deck, to Mombambo's gold pieces. It was easy to see they were trying to persuade him that a few ornaments were little enough to give for the rare wine. But Mombambo kept shaking his head.

"Bring me the copper trinkets from below," Merbal said to Abu. "The necklace of beads, and two of the bracelets." When they were brought, Merbal held them up so Mombambo could see them. There was still fire on the beach, and by the light of it the glow of the copper was just as lovely as gold, Jared thought. Of course it did not have even a small part of the value of gold, but these savages did not seem to know it.

Mombambo pushed his followers aside and came to the water's edge, stripping off his collar and bangles. He put his huge foot upon them, pointed to the wine jars on the deck, and held up ten fingers twice. Merbal did not move; he stood where Mombambo could plainly see him, and his face was disdainful. The bundles of ivories were laid beside the ornaments. Merbal nodded. It was a bargain.

"But we do not have a score of jars left to pay them with," Bela quavered.

Merbal laughed. "Do you think I would waste more of our fine wine on these beasts? We will fetch the gold and the ivories with all possible speed. You Kalab—and you, Michael —and you—" He selected ten of the toughest of the seamen. "I will lead you. Put your daggers in your belts before you go. Eben, do you and the oarsmen bring the ship only close enough so we can wade through the water. Be ready to take it out again on the instant."

Jared climbed down the ladder after the others, though his name had not been called. The flute was still in Mombambo's hand. He had to try to make the chieftain see how precious it was to him.

Kalab and another, waist deep in water, carried the bundles of ivory to the ship. The rest formed a guard for them at the water's edge. Mombambo kept his foot on the ornaments, waiting for Merbal to carry out his end of the trade and deliver the wine jars. The shipmaster stepped up to him with the copper trinkets in his hand. Suddenly he slashed the Nubian across the face with the copper beads, and Mombambo, surprised, unsteady with wine, staggered back in spite of his bigness. The shipmaster snatched up the golden jewels and leapt for the ship's gangway. Jared pounced upon his pipe, which Mombambo had dropped. By the time the chieftain, slow-witted from drunkenness and the blow, realized that he was being cheated, the other shipmen ringed him round with a bristling fence of sharp blades. He bellowed like an angry bull, and a knife flashed in his own hand. Michael, clutching his belly, fell gurgling into the water. Jared saw how the bubbles grew slowly crimson. He tried to lift Michael up, but the older man was much too heavy. Eli, coming to his aid, said, "It is no use—Michael is dead."

Merbal hoarsely ordered the men to push the galley free and come aboard. A few strokes of the oars and it was out of reach of the knives of the savages.

"It is lucky they did not arm themselves with spears, or escape would not have been so easy," Eben said.

Merbal chuckled at the howls of rage which were fast

fading away in the distance. He rubbed his hands. This was the finest trade he had so far made: the valuable ivory and the gold ornaments besides. They had cost nothing but the wine consumed during the feast. And now he had positive proof that more gold lay to the south.

CHAPTER ELEVEN

Unfair Punishment

DO NOT the Zidonians keep any commandments to deal justly with their fellow man?" Jared said to Eben, horrified. "The shipmaster is a cheat and a murderer. Does he not care at all that Michael was killed?"

"I grieve for Michael," Eli said. "He was of my own tribe, and the kindest and best of men. He came on this voyage only out of loyalty to the King, and often said how he longed to be peacefully at home. He hoped this would be his last voyage."

"Well, it was his last voyage," Ira said glumly.

Into their conversation, Kalab cut sharply. "Michael was a good fellow—but such are the fortunes of voyages. There are always risks to be taken for gain. We Phoenicians know that. We do not fight for the glory of Yahveh, like you Hebrews, Eli. If by chance one or two lives are lost, that cannot be helped. We are the greatest traders in the world."

"And not always known for our honesty," Eben said.

"What was dishonest?" Abu said. "Did not the savages get rare wine and a feast? Why do they deserve more?"

"The shipmaster merely gave them the wine to befuddle them, so they could more readily be cheated," Eben said.

"And a very good trick it was," Abu said. "I do not expect the boy to have sense, but you, Eben, should have the shrewdness to recognize this."

"Shrewdness is not everything," Eben said.

"You had better not let the shipmaster hear you criticize his behavior," Abu said.

Merbal ordered the goods to be taken below for storage. He himself carried the gold ornaments. Jared followed him, laden with ivories. Up forward, where the cargo was stowed, they found untidy confusion. The awning which covered the merchandise had been partly ripped away; beads and trinkets and spice jars were scattered everywhere.

Merbal turned on Jared furiously. "So—you have been prying again! The wine for which I sent you was stored on deck. You had no reason to go below. You know very well that no one is permitted to touch the merchandise. What were you after, you young scoundrel?"

"Nothing!" Jared cried. "I did not do this, shipmaster—please believe me."

"Who else could it have been? You were alone on the ship. Every other man was on shore. I thought you had learned not to poke your nose into matters that were not your business. But no; this was your chance to take something for yourself, no doubt; something you could trade for your own profit at the next marketplace. I should have guessed why you were so long returning with the wine. Can you deny that you came below?"

"No, I—" Jared fell silent. He *had* stepped down into the hold for a moment, to imprison Methuselah, the monkey.

Merbal, in his rage, did not hear the twittering from behind one of the chests, but Jared heard it. He saw the bright eyes of the monkey peering out at him. Methuselah squeezed himself from under the heaped merchandise at Merbal's back, ran on hands and knees beneath the feet of the oarsmen, and swung himself through the hatch to the deck. Merbal did not notice.

"It was—" Jared began. But Methuselah looked so frightened, so like the way he himself had felt as a small boy when he had done something he knew to be wrong and had been caught at it. Jared could not bear to accuse the monkey while Merbal was in the midst of one of his furious tempers.

"Strip the boy!" Merbal directed Kalab. "We shall see what he has taken."

Jared struggled helplessly in the arms of the powerful seaman. Kalab held him while Abu tore off his girdle and tunic. When he was naked, Kalab threw him to his knees, twisting his arms so that Jared cried out. Merbal shook the pieces of clothing and kicked them aside. "So you were not even clever enough to find anything," he jeered. "I have been easy with you, but now I am going to teach you to obey orders properly." He picked up a leather thong and brought it down on the boy's back. The whip sent a shiver of agony through Jared. It descended again and again, cutting the flesh. Jared writhed under it, and the tears rolled down his cheeks. He tried to be a man, not to cry out or show how he suffered. It was not only the sore hurt, but the shame of being down on his knees, beaten like the meanest slave, like an animal. He clamped his teeth on his lower lip till the blood came there too, but at last an unwilling, half-strangled yelp escaped him.

Eben leapt down the ladder, pushing aside the men gathered round. "Stop!" he shouted to the shipmaster. "Do you want to kill the boy?"

Merbal swung the lash again. Eben seized his wrist and

held it there. Long trained in the mastery of steering oars that fought against him with the strength of many men, he had a grip of iron. The whip dropped from Merbal's fingers. Eben flung Merbal's arm away. Merbal drew himself up. His face was purple. "Does the helmsman dare to tell me how to discipline my own crew? The boy is a sneak thief!"

"The boy has been punished enough, whatever he did," Eben answered.

"That is for me to say," Merbal said coldly. "The boy has been punished enough for now—yes. Let the helmsman return to his post."

The two glared at one another; then, seeing that the shipmaster made no attempt to pick up the whip again, Eben stalked away.

Jared was still on his knees, holding his hands before his face, choking back the sobs. The raw pain of his back seemed to reach from his toes to his teeth. "That is only a taste of what you will get if you do not heed me," Merbal said. "Now pick up the goods you strewed about in your careless haste and then get out of here—get out of the hold, do you understand?—and if you ever come here again without my orders, you may not live to regret it!"

Jared crawled about collecting each last bead and trinket, even those that had rolled far away under the benches. He was aware of the oarsmen watching him, some curious, some in pity. Even those who might be indignant did not dare speak up lest they draw the shipmaster's anger upon themselves. At last everything was restored to its proper place. The ivories and gold ornaments were stowed in chests, and the awning tied down over all. Merbal took up the clay tablets upon which he did his accounts, and had a lighted lamp brought to him upon the prow.

It was a windless night; the oarsmen rowed steadily, and the ship glided through the black water on an even keel. Jared picked up his clothes and limped, stiff and sore, to the poop deck. The other shipmen crowded around, but Eben waved them away. "Let him have air and quiet."

Telling Eli to hold the steering oar steady, he fetched olive oil and gently smoothed it on the bleeding welts that the thong had made. "It was foolish to take upon yourself the guilt of an ape," Eben said, when Jared had told him what had happened.

"Yes, I know," Jared said. "But Merbal might have killed Methuselah. And he might not have believed me even if I *had* spoken. He hates me."

"It is easily seen that the shipmaster does not like you," Eben said. "I have not been able to reason out why."

"He says I am useless," Jared said.

"That is false talk. Every ship needs someone to perform the tasks you do. And in addition, you have been quick at learning the work of a grown shipman." Eben scratched his chin reflectively. "The shipmaster calls you 'freedom lover' sometimes, does he not?"

Jared nodded, remembering how Merbal had heard his plea for freedom at the judgment of Solomon, and how scornful he had been of it.

"Merbal would prefer to have slaves for a crew," Eben said. "He does his best to make those on this galley slaves to his will, at least for the voyage. And he knows you Hebrews are a stiff-necked, rebellious folk. But still, such venom as he vents on you—"

Jared's back hurt him too much for deep thought on the problem. Or for further talk, either. He shook his head dumbly.

"The shipmaster is plagued with demons," Eben said. "Why should he accuse you of stealing? The demon of avarice has twisted his mind so that he no longer sees reason. All he cares about are the spices, the ivory, the gold. Is his passion for these only for the sake of praise and reward from the King? I wonder!"

He paused, cupping his hand to his ear.

Jared was listening too. "Is it thunder?" he asked. The sky was clear, the stars glittering. There was no sign of storm east, west, north, or south. Yet a dull, ominous thumping followed the ship across the water from the direction of Mombambo's village.

"It is the drums," Eben said. "Listen how they roll—now fast, now slow—over and over again with the same beat to the rhythm as if it were saying something for others to hear."

The shipmen who were sleeping on the deck roused and began to listen too. It was a fearful sound to hear in the dark of the night, by the lonely shores of Africa, so far away from home.

"It is a message," Eben said.

"To us?" Eli asked.

"No, not to us. Mombambo is warning other chieftains and tribes not to deal with us—perhaps to slaughter us if we appear at their villages."

"How far will the drums be heard?" Eli asked.

"Farther than you think. We are many furlongs away, and yet the drums woke you from your slumber."

Merbal blew out his lamp and walked aft. Jared retreated hastily into the shadow of the bulwarks. "Helmsman, what do you make of that sound?" Merbal asked.

The sound was the roar of an angry, wounded lion—a dangerous lion to encounter.

"It is the war drums," Eben said. "Mombambo is passing the word from village to village of what we did this night."

"Ignorant, drunken savages!" Merbal growled. "Their own gluttony allowed me to make the better bargain."

"That was no bargain," Eben said. "The shipmaster himself knows it was outright thieving."

"So—you dare again to pass judgment on my behavior!" Merbal shouted. "I will have you thrown into chains for your boldness!"

"I will do you little good in chains," Eben said. "Michael is dead; there is no other trained at the steering oars. How will you bring this galley to your land of gold without a helmsman?"

It was too dark to see Merbal's face, but it was easy to see, by the way he stood, with hunched shoulders and swinging, apelike arms, how angry he was.

Eben bowed; whether in mock humility or not, Jared could not tell. "Merbal is the servant of King Solomon," Eben said. "Eben too is the servant of King Solomon. As such Eben will perform his duties faithfully to the end of the voyage. But if the boy is unfairly molested, I will take his part, I warn you."

"Enough of this talk," Merbal growled. "Do your duty and I will let you pamper this puppy for whatever mistaken reasons you may have. But do not tell me how to run my ship, or I will take the helm myself. There is no one on a ship that cannot be spared, except the shipmaster." He walked away.

"Must we starve and thirst again or be slaughtered if we try to land?" Bela wailed. "Oh, why will the shipmaster not turn back at last?"

"When he has only a few trinkets of gold thus far?" Eli

said. "Do you remember what he promised us? A land where the rivers run with gold—that's what he expects to find. And he will never turn back till he finds it, though we all die first."

"The shipmaster knows as well as I do that the ship is foul with moss and the sail so worn and patched that the first storm will rip it again completely," Eben said. "Merbal will have no ship left under him if he does not soon reach a port where there are skilled workmen and supplies." He added, so low that only Jared, crouched at his feet, could hear him, "There is something brewing in the shipmaster's mind. What it is, I have not yet been able to understand."

CHAPTER TWELVE

Shores of Africa

FOR a time Jared got no more kicks or cuffs and very little abuse. "It is because you have championed me," he told the helmsman.

"Merbal acts sweet as honey and smooth as olive oil because he cannot get along without me," Eben answered. "He is master of the ship, and I will do my duty, but he is not my friend."

Merbal's next attempt to trade was as disastrous as Eben had predicted. No sooner were the goods laid out on the shore and the signal fire lit, than spears flew from the village stockade. One stuck, quivering, in a bale of goods on the deck, and Jared knew it might just as well have pierced himself or his comrades. Merbal shouted to Yshmael, and the oarsmen quickly took the galley out of range. But the trade goods had to be left behind, and the shipmaster was angry, even though this happened because of his own treachery.

"So much fuss over the loss of a few baubles!" Eli said.

Peleg, who had a mind for business, answered, "It is the loss of trade that the shipmaster regrets."

The hold of the ship was already uncomfortably cluttered

with all the stuff Merbal had gathered here and there, and the shipmen did not care if trading was suspended, so long as they were not driven too hard. Merbal was wooing the good will not only of Eben but of all the crew. Constantly he reminded them of the golden rewards that lay ahead, and almost every day the galley landed for the sake of rest and refreshment. These now had to be lonely spots where no one lived, tiny islets where plentiful waterfowl were easily slaughtered, and fish were caught in baskets between the tides. The eggs of sea turtles nesting on the beach were considered a special delicacy. There were groves of wild mangos, and custard apples. Jared particularly liked the white meat and milk of the coconut; Methuselah would shinny up the tall palm trees and shake down the fruit for his friend.

Yet they were all glad to see civilization again when the galley came to a Sheban colony of which Merbal had learned from the merchants of Hazarmaveth. The seal which Solomon had entrusted to Merbal, the insignia of the Sheban Queen entwined with his own, acted as a passport to the governor of the town. The galley was careened on the beach, and Jared now learned much about the care of vessels. With the others he worked to clean the bottom of the sea moss and worms that had collected over months of travel, till his own knuckles were scraped almost clean of skin. Eben said the tiny sea creatures were so ferocious that if left alone, they would eat away the wood of the ship till it was as full of leaks as a wicker basket.

Jared learned how to stuff tow into the seams between the planks, and further make them tight with pitch drawn from the pine tree. A fire was kindled on the beach; wax was melted and added to tar and paint, and the whole outer hull of the galley given a fresh coat of this mixture. Mean-

while, expert Sheban sailmakers of the town were stitching a
new sail.

After their hours of work, the shipmen found companions
and amusement in the town. Even Eben said, "A man must
have some pleasures ashore or he becomes covered with
barnacles too, like a ship on a long voyage." Sometimes he
took Jared with him, but the boy soon grew tired of the
bazaars to which the hunters of Kush brought ivory and
skins and ostrich feathers. Being quick-witted, he amused
himself by picking up a knowledge of the Sheban tongue.

It was spring, the month of Nissan, when the *Mekada* left
port again with a fair wind behind her. She was well stocked
with fresh food and drinking water and the crew were in fine
humor after their rest ashore. So long as things went well,
they grumbled neither against the shipmaster for his greedy
haste, nor against Eben for risking the displeasure of
Melkarth and Astoreth by his lack of reverence.

Merbal promised the crew wonderful things. With wine
he had loosened the tongues of the Sheban merchants and
shipmasters of the port and they had told him that there was
gold—much gold—in the south. Though Jared feared and
hated the shipmaster, he wanted to see the land where the
gold grew too. His fears were renewed because Merbal had
brought aboard an addition to the crew which made Eben's
situation, and his own, less favorable than before. It was
Jobab, a Sheban helmsman, to take Michael's place in as-
sisting Eben.

He was an amiable fellow, with a sly secret smile always
in his black eyes. His oiled ringlets, long lashes, and smooth
olive skin would have made him appear womanish if it had
not been for the broad shoulders and bulging arm muscles
that came from years of wrestling with the steering oars.

Jared did not like the new helmsman; Eben had been training Eli to help him and there seemed little reason for Jobab's
presence—unless it was to make Merbal independent of
Eben. But when Jared voiced these doubts, Eben answered,
"Jobab has expert knowledge of African waters and of the
Sheban colonies along this coast. Merbal has use for such
a one."

It was Jobab who told the crew of the ship's destination.
"It is Havilah, near the southern tip of Africa, a land which
is honeycombed with golden rock, and the port of Tharshish,
from which the gold of the mines is shipped to Sheba." He
added, with his eyes gleaming like pools of marsh water in
the sun, "If we carry away even a small part of that gold, we
shall all be rich—rich as the courtiers of the Queen."

Jared thought this was a wild story like the ones that Eli
delighted in telling. Even if it were true, the gold was the
property of the Sheban queen; therefore why should King
Solomon's shipmen grow rich from it? That Merbal would
manage to get some of the gold, he did not doubt; and a small
reward for each shipman, such as Merbal had promised,
seemed reasonable enough. He wondered if Merbal would
give him *his* share. It would be too bad to go through all
these perils and bring nothing home to his mother Mara.

Jared had two new playmates to take his mind off trouble,
two doves which Jobab had brought on board with him to
help him, so he said, in navigation. He was glad to give Jared
the care of them. Jared cleaned their cage, fed them barley
grains and water, whistled at them and they answered back.
But since he was not Solomon, he could not understand
their language. Methuselah was jealous of them, and Jared
had to keep close watch lest the monkey stick his paw between the bars of the cage and do the birds harm. With all

his tasks, time passed swiftly for the boy. The wind blew steady and strong, and even though Osh, the North Star, was not visible so far south, Eben was satisfied that the ship was headed in the right direction. Merbal allowed a landing every day or so but he did no trading. Between times, they were often out of sight of land entirely.

One day Eben called to Jobab. "Cast your eyes on the brown streaks that wander through the blue. Is it not river water?"

"Indeed Eben is a wise navigator," Jobab said. "The great stream at the mouth of which lies the port of Tharshish sends its waters far out into the sea. I have been watching for them, but Eben's eyes discovered them first. Let us make sure in which direction the shore lies." He fetched his cage and set the doves free. They hovered over the deck for a moment, trying out their wings that had been unused for so long. It seemed to Jared as if they waved goodby before they flew off one after the other. Eben swung the ship's nose to follow them. They were land birds, looking for their homes, and they would guide the ship to the shore.

Peleg, up on the yardarm, cried out that a ship was approaching. It was deep in the water and, unlike the *Mekada*, not decked over, so that Jared could see the black-skinned oarsmen tugging at their heavy load. Their oars flashed in perfect time to a sad, monotonous chant. The sun was reflected for a moment from metal shackles on wrist and ankle. The wake of the galley arrowed away toward a break in the fever-green jungle, and the shore breeze smelled of swamps.

When the sail was furled, the *Mekada* was taken under oars into a wide bay rimmed with mangrove trees whose serpentine roots grew from the water. Feeling the way with a lead line, Merbal made across the bay for the town, which

was heavily guarded by walls and watchtowers. The shipmaster ordered all to remain aboard save himself and Jobab.

While the rest of the crew waited, Jared amused himself
by tootling on his flute. He had been teaching Methuselah to
dance to it, but the monkey was not nearly so graceful as his
goats had been. Jared gave up in disgust and sought the
company of the helmsman. Eben seemed deep in thought.
"Are you doubtful of a friendly reception here?" Jared
asked. "We had no trouble at the other Sheban port."

"To put into a harbor and pay honestly for repairs and
supplies is one thing," Eben said. "To come *demanding* gold
is another. This Tharshish looks more like a fortress than a
free trading center. All the world knows that the Queen of
Sheba allows no ships to carry gold but her own, that she
will let none but her own merchants deal with her colonies.
Merbal's boldness in this venture might be called courage,
but it might also be foolhardy."

"What of the seal he carries, and the alliance that has been
made between Solomon and Sheba?" Eli asked.

Eben looked doubtful. "I did not hear of such a league,
either in Tyre or Ezion-geber. I heard only that Solomon
wished a trade pact."

Eben was right, of course, Jared thought. What exactly
had been Solomon's words when he had handed the seal to
Merbal? He had called it "a sign of the compact I *hope* to
make with her." But Merbal, no doubt, with the help of the
oily-tongued Jobab, would brazen out a plausible tale of an
alliance already settled. Should he tell Eben what Solomon
had actually said? No, Jared decided. Here, in this fortified
Sheban port, all the members of *Mekada's* crew were in grave
danger if Merbal's tale was disbelieved. It would be better
to keep his knowledge to himself till Africa was left behind

forever. And, having come this far, Jared himself wished ardently to see the land of gold.

Merbal and Jobab returned saying that all had gone well. Jobab, in his oily way, had confirmed Merbal's story of being an emissary not only from King Solomon and Hiram of Tyre, but from the Queen of Sheba herself. The governor had given Merbal permission to take the galley upriver to the gold country, and had sent a guide to point out the way. Kalonga was a black man so tall that he dwarfed even Eben. Though he had a savage look, with half-shaved head and teeth filed to points, his manner was dignified and princely—but branded on his forehead was the Sheban slave mark. And Jared saw, to his horror, that Kalonga's right arm was severed at the wrist.

As the oarsmen made for the mouth of the river, Kalonga stood beside Eben giving him directions in the Sheban tongue. Without these, the ship would surely have grounded, or become lost among the many twisting channels and jungle-covered islets. Many great beasts with leathery wrinkled hides were sunning themselves on the banks, rolling playfully in the mud, or swimming in the river. Mother hippos swam with their babies clinging to their necks. And once Jared fell suddenly to the deck as the galley jarred on a submerged bank. Merbal yelled at Kalonga, and looked abashed when a fat black beast heaved up from under the keel with an indignant bellow that showed a gaping red mouth and stumpy yellow teeth. Kalonga laughed at Jared's startled face. "The river horse does not eat men," he said.

The many river outlets merged into one wide channel. The men found it easy to row against the sluggish current, or pole the galley along in the shallows. Just the same, Jared

would have preferred the narrow, rushing Jordan to this oozing stream with its stagnant pools giving off evil vapors.

He went below to do his turn among the rowers. His tunic stuck to his damp skin but he dared not take it off and expose more of himself to the insects. There were thousands of them dancing about. And Jared, tugging away at his oar, could not spare a hand to slap them away.

There was no twilight; the red sun plunged suddenly into the jungle and was smothered. No breeze of evening came to cool the men on the crowded ship, and they despaired of finding a camping place among the dense thickets of bamboo and palm. But Kalonga's practiced eye spotted a clearing made by wild elephants that had torn up trees and trampled on them. The galley was beached on muddy ground criss-crossed with huge footprints; in the distance the elephants could be heard trumpeting a warning to the trespassers. Quickly a fire was kindled from the splintered wood; Merbal sent Jared to gather more sticks from the outskirts of the clearing. It was hard not to drop pieces here and there, and Jared reached for a hanging vine to tie what he had gathered into a bundle. The vine slithered away with a hiss, and Jared dropped all his kindling at once. At the clatter of it, Merbal shouted impatiently for Jared to hurry. So there, on the gloomy edge of the black forest, he had to stoop and pick up the sticks again, not knowing where the serpent was or when it would return.

The cook fire made a pool of safe yellow light, but round about it the jungle was hideous with hoots and whistles. The amber eyes of great cats stared out of the darkness, reflecting the flames. The whole clearing smelled musky as the lair of a mountain lion.

"I do not like this forest or this river," Jared whispered to Eben. "It speaks to me of evil."

Eben motioned that the boy should sleep close by him, and this was comforting, but Jared was glad just the same when dawn came and the monkeys began to chatter, noisy as women in the market place. Methuselah scolded at them in shrill tones from the deck of the galley, where he was tied to keep him out of trouble.

Jared could not shake off his gloom even when he was safe on the galley again. In this jungle man was unfriendly too. The only signs of human life were stone forts at fording places, and villages of empty huts, some blackened by fire, some deserted and falling apart. Seeing the melancholy on Kalonga's face, Jared asked him what had happened here.

"These were simple fisherpeople who knew not the ways of war," Kalonga said. "They were easily taken prisoner by the white men from across the sea. Even my own tribe, that are warriors, had no weapons to match the iron swords of the Shebans. The white men gave us promises of peace which they did not keep when we laid down our spears. They killed or made harmless the leaders and enslaved the people." He held up his maimed arm. "A beast of burden can be useful so, but what can a warrior do without a fighting hand?"

Jared looked at the scarred stump and looked away again, feeling his stomach turn over. "I was a slave once," he said, "I know—a little—what it is like."

"Then we are friends," Kalonga said. "Did you too work at the gold mines?"

Jared shook his head, but he thought that it was of little importance to a slave whether he labored for gold or copper, or just to make a life of ease for his masters.

"It was because of the gold that the Shebans came and took our homeland from us," Kalonga said. "It was because of the gold that they enslaved us. I curse the gold!"

Jared looked at the wild country stretching far away along the river bank. "Can't you escape?"

"There are too many guards. Have you not seen how your master has me watched and my feet tied, one to the other, each night?"

Jared had been thinking only of his own fears; he had not noticed the other's suffering.

"Even if I somehow managed to break away," Kalonga said, "there are Sheban forts everywhere along the river and the forest paths. But I still hope, and watch for a chance of freedom."

After some days, Kalonga said the rest of the journey must be afoot. Merbal picked out several men to guard the ship and told the rest to make ready to march inland. They were to carry gifts for the Queen's consul at Zimbabwe, the Place of the Mines, and on the return trip to carry out the gold. He named Jared among these: "You will have to see if you can't carry as much as the others, for I do not trust you enough to leave you with the cargo."

Jared picked up Methuselah. Merbal snapped, "No monkey friends for you on this journey, my boy! The beast could not help where *we* are going. Are you afraid?"

Jared shot him a look of dislike and turned to tie up Methuselah, and pet him, promising to come back soon. He *was* afraid, but nothing would have made him admit it.

"I will go too," Eben said.

"Why not?" Merbal answered. Jobab was also of the party; there was no need of a helmsman on the ship as long as it was drawn up on shore. Kalab was left in charge of it. He promised to treat Methuselah well, but the monkey's sad eyes followed Jared down the gangway.

After the men had all adjusted their burdens, Kalonga

showed the way to a path which ran along a small branch of the river. When they came to a ford, Kalonga warned them to step carefully through the shallows; there were crocodiles here that would take a man's leg off at a single bite. This was something more definite than the mysterious dangers of Zimbabwe or the perils of the sea to which the shipmen were accustomed. No one wanted to be the first to wade across.

Merbal fumed and called them all cowards. "See, I will show you!" Disdainfully he splashed through the stream, hardly looking where he put his feet. Kalonga, close behind, yanked him to one side, just as what had seemed to be a floating log snapped open a long red jaw full of needle-sharp teeth. Merbal paled, but kept going to the opposite bank.

"You must grant that the shipmaster is a brave man, even though a hard one," Eli said. "He knows we must follow if we are not to be ashamed." But still he hesitated.

Eben crossed over next, picking his way carefully and calmly in just the same fashion as he steered the *Mekada* among coral reefs. Jared tagged in his wake. And so did the others, one by one, till they were all safely across. The crocodile raised itself, opening its jaws and leering at them, disappointed.

Merbal strode ahead down the path. Kalonga was waiting to see that all passed over the stream safely. "You might have escaped more easily if you had let the beast get Merbal," Jared said, shuddering. He could not wish such a fate to anyone, but he wondered at Kalonga's behavior.

"I would not throw a man to the River Devil even to save my own life. But this shipman will soon see that the masters of Zambabwe are as wicked as any crocodile," Kalonga said.

CHAPTER THIRTEEN

The Land of Gold

THE landing party followed ruts made by heavy-laden bullock carts through the jungle. Spotted guinea fowl started up with queer harsh cries; monkeys jabbered, and Jared felt better. He was climbing upward toward blue hills; the weather had become brisk and sunny-bright as an early autumn day in Judah. He wrinkled up his short nose and sniffed, hoping to find the familiar sweetness of ripening grapes on the upland wind.

The groves thinned as the hills drew close around the path, and the rough slopes were pitted with quarries and worked-out mine shafts. The shipmaster's black beard was positively bristling with joy as he scooped up a handful of pebbles from a dry stream bed and saw that they were pure quartz—a sure sign of gold country. He pushed his heavy body up an incline of sliding shale to examine the broken rock heaps at the mouth of an abandoned tunnel. His hands were shaking when he showed a sample of it to Abu. "There will be richer where we are going," he said and tossed it aside.

Jared snatched up the stone and held it to the sun. The flecks of metal in it sparkled. Merbal seemed to think it not worth keeping, but Merbal was a greedy one. Jared would be satisfied with just a little bit of gold to take to Mara, so he stuffed it in his girdle, where it made a lump as big as a hen's egg and much more uncomfortable, rubbing against his belly.

Kalonga signaled for a halt and trotted ahead out of sight. Jared puzzled over the sound that came from the direction he had taken. It was a familiar sound which warmed the boy's heart. Often at home he had wakened to hear this grating of stone on stone as his mother and the other women of his village ground meal for the morning bread cakes. The sound was so loud and steady that it must come from a very big village indeed. There was the merry song of a running stream as well. Kalonga shouted and a man's voice answered him, but the grinding never stopped. Kalonga reappeared between the trees and beckoned. "I have told the captain of the guard that you come; otherwise he would kill you before asking why."

They came to a clearing beside a river. Perched on the banks and on boulders in the middle of the stream were many half-naked blacks, both men and women. The rock ledges along the stream were pock-marked with hundreds of grinding holes, but it was not grain that they were grinding. They were crushing quartz with round stone mortars. The powder they washed from the crumbled fragments was yellow as butter, and shining like the sun—gold!

Jared hardly had time to take this in before his party was surrounded by armed guards. He knew they must be Shebans because they were the only white men. The captain said impatiently, "Be on your way! We do not welcome strangers here, whether they bear a permit from the port governor or no." He cracked his whip viciously when a woman slave slowed her grinding for a moment to look up. The other slaves muttered; that was all they dared to do. There were

many more of them than there were Shebans, but the white
masters were heavily armed, and the slaves were without
weapons, and by the looks of them, weak with starvation
and overwork.

Merbal hurried his men across the clearing. Their eyes
bulged at glimpses of gold dust in clay vessels and heaps of
gold-veined rock beside a fire where it was being roasted to
soften it before grinding.

"What riches these Shebans must have!" Merbal said to
Abu. "Did you see how even the common soldiers had swords
inlaid with gold and spears with gold-decorated handles?
There is more treasure here than I ever dreamed of!"

"But can *we* get our hands on it?" Abu said. "These fellows
do not seem easy to deal with."

"The captain of a slave guard must necessarily be a hard
man," Merbal said. "The consul at Zimbabwe, the Queen's
own agent, is bound to be more worldly, more open to per-
suasion—one who knows the ways of trade."

The shipmen were full of misgivings. They were unarmed,
for Merbal had wished thus to prove his peaceful intentions.
Only Jared knew the full story of Merbal's dishonesty, but
others, after the incident with Mombambo, feared that the
shipmaster's behavior might bring trouble upon them.

"As long as the ship is close at my back, I am willing to
face danger," Eli said. "But it is a long way through the
forest to our galley now; should the Shebans turn against us
we would never get away." He shifted uncomfortably under
his bundle of trade goods. "Not only do we go unarmed and
outnumbered in hostile country, but we are beasts of burden
besides. I did not join up for this sort of service."

"The rewards will be worth it," Peleg said.

"You, Peleg, have caught the fever from the shipmaster," Eli said. "You would do anything for gold, wouldn't you?"

"Since when are *you* grown so noble?" Peleg asked.

"I wouldn't thieve for it," Eli said. "Mind you, I'm not accusing the shipmaster of robbing the Shebans, but he'd be willing to."

"Close your mouths, both of you," Eben said. "If Merbal does not have the authority he claims, he will no doubt make some honest arrangement about any gold we take aboard the galley."

Jared was relieved to hear Eben say this. He was too tired to care much about the argument, however. The earthenware wine jug he carried strapped on his shoulders chafed his skin, and the weight of it gave him the backache. And the unhappy slaves, the brutal faces of the Sheban guards, the wildness of the country, the thousands of leagues between it and home—all of these things weighed on him even more heavily.

The road they followed now ran through a river gorge between walls of rock. Jared was stumbling badly by the time they came out into a wide valley rimmed with high mountains. It looked peaceful as the valleys of Israel, checkered with the bright colors of grain fields and orchards. Then he saw a huge stone fortress frowning down upon him from a table mountain. It stood high enough to command the approach to the valley, and by the time the men reached its base, a company of soldiers had come from behind the huge boulders that screened the ascent. Kalonga delivered the message from the port governor; Merbal bowed low before the captain of the company. Before he could straighten up, he was seized by guards. Jared's pleasure at the sight of the shipmaster's discomfort ended quickly as the soldiers laid hands on the rest of them.

Kalonga was led away to the slave quarters. He made no resistance.

"Search the strangers," said the Sheban captain.

The shipmen were glad to give up their burdens. But Eli and some of the others were roughly treated when it was discovered that they had knives and slingshots concealed in their garments. Jared feared that he would be punished for a thief when the lump of ore was found in his girdle. But the soldier who was searching him laughed and tossed the bit of rock away.

"What sort of a reception is this for one who comes as the messenger of King Solomon and Sheba?" Merbal bellowed. "Your Queen shall hear of this insult to my person!"

"Tell your story to the consul in the hall of the great temple," the Sheban captain answered curtly. "Now get on with you—all of you—in single file."

Jared stumbled up the steep stone steps that zigzagged across one side of the hill. The other three were sheer precipices, and the course of the river had been changed to circle round the base. This was a place that could be defended against any number of attackers. But that wasn't what made it so frightening. There was something else about it; something Jared couldn't put his finger on. A ring wall sprang from the upper rim of the rock, twice as thick as the height of a man, and made of blocks so huge that many scores of slaves must have struggled to put them in place. The sun was setting directly behind the black ramparts as he toiled upward, edging them with crimson light. Eli, directly in front of him, panted out, "Who cares for the name of King Solomon here? I tell you, I feel doom in my bones! I'd rather be back on that island with the three-headed men!" Jared had never seen three-headed men, but he also felt that he would prefer them to the temple-fortress of Zimbabwe.

The line of men squeezed through a narrow wall opening into a maze of curved passages. Jared tried to memorize the twists and turns of the corridors in case there should be a chance later to escape, but no one could hope to find a way out of here. Passing through a labyrinth of courtyards, he bumped along in a pitch-black tunnel between dank walls, treading on the heels of Eli in the haste born of dread. The echoing footsteps of his companions failed to drown out sounds from the cellars below: the blows of hammers, the clang of metal; the crack of a whip, muffled cries. A whiff of smoke smelled of smelting furnaces.

But the stone floor sloped upward and the sounds faded off beneath their feet. Slowly the vaulted passage filled with rosy light, and the prisoners came out on a roofless egg-shaped platform overlooking the whole valley. Jared knew this was a heathen temple. Hunched, misshapen birds, eagles and vultures, looked down from columns of hewn stone, over-laid with golden symbols of sun, moon, and stars. A cone-shaped tower soared up behind a stone altar stained with red —whether because of the sunset light or from some other dread reason, Jared could not tell.

The passageways rumbled with the sound of chanting and the clash of cymbals. From a hidden portal behind the tower crawled a golden serpent of warriors in gleaming armor, priests in robes that glittered and flashed as they moved. They walked slowly, weighted down with their ornaments. One priest, unable to support himself, was carried in a golden chair by two black slaves.

Jerah, the consul, was a powerful man with a dark, handsome face. His white tunic, threaded with gold, was cut short and sleeveless, the better to display the bangles circling his muscular legs and arms. His voice boomed across the valley: "What do the strangers want in the Sacred City of the Mines?"

Merbal answered him boldly. "I come from far away, from Ezion-geber on the Sea called Red, to look upon the wonders of your great Queen's Empire and to bring back gold to her partner and friend, King Solomon of Israel."

"I have been told of no such partnership," the consul said.

Merbal stretched out his hand with the seal in it. "See how the signs of Solomon and Sheba are entwined as a proof of their love. The Queen wishes Solomon to have whatever he desires. And I am he who is to bring it to him."

His greed gives Merbal the courage of a lion, Jared thought.

The consul turned the seal over and over in his hand. "This is not proof enough of a league between my Queen and your King. I have never seen a seal like unto this one; it may be a forgery—"

The Sheban helmsman, Jobab, fell on his knees before the consul, knocked his forehead against the earth three times, and singsonged: "Oh noble my lord Jerah, this your servant dares to speak to you as one come lately from the court of great Queen Bilkis. She bids me recommend this brave shipmaster to you with the words of my mouth—"

Jared could see the consul tapping his gold-sandaled foot impatiently till finally he pushed the groveling Jobab with it and interrupted: "The words of your mouth slide out too easily, my fellow countryman—I have no faith in them or you."

He turned instead to the priest who sat in the golden carrying chair, an ancient dwarfish man with a yellow and

twisted face, and a goat beard tangled among ropes of gold
beads. "Uzal, High Priest of the Temple, tell us: what is the
will of the Queen?"

"I will tell you—" Merbal began again.

"Silence!" The priest screamed in a high-pitched voice
that scraped against the ears like a file. "You are in the presence of the gods! Fiery Dat-Hamim, the Sun, is sinking to
rest, but already Ilmkh, the Moon, is rising, and when dawn
comes, Attar, the Morning Star, will look down upon you.
These are the gods whom we must consult; *they* will tell us
the Queen's will. What have you brought as a sacrifice to the
gods of Sheba?"

"I brought many rich gifts," Merbal said. "They were taken
from me at the portal."

The consul made a sign, and Merbal's goods were spread
upon the pavement. The things looked pitifully few and
cheap in this place where gold was commoner than brass
was among the Israelites. There were a few bars of raw
copper; some brazen basins, pitchers, and cups; some honey
and wine and olive oil in jars stained with salt water and tar
from the ship. It would have been better to offer nothing,
Jared thought. Gods demanded burnt offerings: fat bullocks
and lambs.

"I speak not of worldly goods," the priest said scornfully.
"Did you not bring a fair youth to give to Attar, the God of
the Morning Star, who watches over his sacred Zimbabwe?"

Jared gasped, and a cold shiver ran down his back. Eben
had told him of babies sacrificed to the Zidonian gods; he
himself had heard rumors of human sacrifice among the
Canaanites who dwelt near to Judah. But he had never quite
believed these tales.

The consul looked sternly on Merbal. "The priest Uzal

has spoken true: it is Attar that will tell us whether it is his will for you to receive our gold."

The priest, screaming and frothing at the lips, was pointing a bony finger towards Jared. The boy shrank back, trying first to hide behind the others; then to blow himself up, to stretch so that he would appear as big as they.

"*There* is the youth!" shrieked the priest. "Let them offer him up to Attar if they wish to prove that they come in good faith."

Jared's knees gave way as two priestly attendants seized him by the arms and began to drag him towards the altar. He was having an evil dream surely, from which he would wake in time. As through a veil he heard his comrades murmuring in horror.

The consul stroked his small, neatly trimmed beard, looking Jared over for signs of deformity or blemish which would make him unsuitable for sacrifice. But there were none, for though Jared did not know it, he was a fair youth indeed. His limbs had grown round and strong from the work of the ship; the sea wind had tanned him with a rosy glow that made his eyes very blue; and his dark hair, damp with the sweat of fear, curled in ringlets on his shapely head. Jerah's face flickered with a moment of pity. "Let us not be too hasty, Uzal," he said to the priest. "The boy cannot be sacrificed till the Star rises at dawn. We shall first bind him upon the altar for this night, and in the morning, the spirit of Attar will enter his body, and speak truth to us."

"Let me go! Let me go!" Jared cried out. The valley echoed with his cry. His struggles were useless. Eben hurled himself upon the attendants. "All the gold in the world is not worth such a sacrifice!" he shouted. "Shipmaster, tell the consul we wish no treasure! Set the boy free!"

The consul held up his hand, waiting. When Merbal was silent, Eben was seized also. "He who crosses the will of Attar's servants must also meet with the god," Jerah said. "This man too shall be bound upon the altar."

And Abu muttered, "The mocker of gods will see now what it is like to be in their power."

CHAPTER FOURTEEN

The Temple of the Morning Star

EBEN and Jared, bound hand and foot, lay side by side
on the altar of stones. The moon, full and round, sailed
overhead. Never had the moon seemed less beautiful. Yet
when Jared closed his eyes against its light, his mind called
up images more terrifying even than the great carved birds
on the columns, or the long blue shadows across the
pavement. A smoking golden bowl filled the air with the
smell of burning incense and myrrh, but it did not smell
sweet to Jared. He tried not to let Eben feel his shaking,
but they lay too close for it to be concealed.

"Will the heathen god make me speak the truth aloud?"
Jared quavered. "For the truth is that Merbal is lying. There
is no league between Solomon and Sheba."

"I suspected as much," Eben said. "Yet if you confess this,
all the shipmen—not just we two—will be killed."

"I do not want to say it. But suppose I am moonstruck?
Suppose by the time the morning star rises, I babble against
my will?"

"I have spent many a night under the moon and never
lost my wits from it," Eben said. "That is a tale the priests
use to frighten innocents. Surely you do not believe in the
Sheban gods?"

Jared twitched in his bonds and his foot struck against cold metal. It was the gold-handled sacrificial knife which Uzal, the High Priest, had laid upon the altar, saying that Attar had the power to wield it himself if he pleased. Jared moaned, and Eben guessed what he was thinking. "What can a god that is not real do to us?" Eben said. "In the morning when the star rises and the consul finds us here still alive, he will set us free."

"*If* we are still alive," Jared said, very low.

"Pray to your just and powerful Yahweh to save us both," Eben said.

Jared prayed, but he seemed to have little faith in the Lord that night; the pagan gods seemed too close and real. He turned and twisted his head, which was the only part of himself that he could move freely, and tried not to moan aloud again. Because he was so much shorter than Eben, his face was on a level with the helmsman's hands, which were twisted across his chest and tied down to golden rings on the altar. Jared's mouth brushed across the harsh strands of the rope that bound them. And the Lord answered his prayer, for an idea came to him. Like all mountain people nourished on milk and curds and cheese, Jared's teeth were strong and sharp. He would gnaw away Eben's bonds till his hands were free, and then Eben would be able to reach for the knife and do the rest. Jared told Eben what he had in mind, and then he set to work as if he were a rat. Every so often when he paused to spit out the shreds of hemp, Eben would jerk and strain till the blood ran from his wrist.

"It is useless," Jared said after a while. "You are hurting yourself, and the rope is so stout I will never bite it through."

"Go on," Eben said. "Chew, bite, gnaw—I would rather the flesh were gnawed from my hands than to remain here helpless like this." Jared knew from his tone that Eben too was doubtful of what the night and the morning might bring. He worked on, though his jaws grew tired and his gums sore.

The moon was low; the middle watch of the night was over, when Eben jerked mightily and broke the last strand. "Oh noble rodent!" he said, and gave Jared's curls a tug before setting to work with the free hand to undo the rope that tied down the other. This too was difficult, and there was another time of near despair before the knot was loosened and Eben could sit up, reach for the knife, and slash his remaining bonds and Jared's.

Jared flexed his numb fingers, stamped his numb feet. "Quiet, quiet!" Eben warned. "We do not know how much longer we shall be alone."

The stings and stabs of blood returning to the limbs were painful, but hope returned too. "What shall we do now?" Jared whispered.

"Wait. I must think. This Zimbabwe is no easy place to run from." Eben walked to the parapet and stood looking down the precipice. It was a sheer drop; even a boy as agile as Jared would be dashed to his death if he attempted to descend it. Beyond the faintly gleaming river at the base, there was the wide valley to be crossed, and beyond that the whole long jungle journey till the ship could be reached. And even there the Shebans could pursue fugitives. Eben beat against his forehead with his fist. "I do not know," he said. "Somehow we *must* find a way."

Far down the stone passageways within the fortress, the tap-tap-tap of footsteps echoed. "One comes," Eben said. "Quick, we will lie as before and pretend we are still tied."

The footsteps crept and stumbled. Jared, holding himself rigid, turned only his head in the direction of the hidden portal. He saw a twisted, batlike form creep from behind the tower and slowly approach the altar, till the dead white face, hollow eyes, a beard made of tangled cobweb, were leaning over him. The shrunken lips mumbled madly. The skinny hands fumbled; they touched Jared's skin and it became goose flesh. Then the hands found what they were hunting: the sacrificial knife.

Jared lay paralyzed, but Eben leapt up and seized the arm that was just raising the knife to kill. The killer resisted with uncanny strength, but Eben bent the arm till the knife turned against the creature's own breast. The body dropped in a crumpled heap of black draperies with a pool of blood spreading from it. It was Uzal, the High Priest.

Eben stood silently looking down at the dead man. "I do not like to kill. But a mad animal must be put out of the way. This priest, possessed by evil, thought to kill us and claim it was the god's work."

The sky was beginning to grow light in the east. The stars of night were fading, but a single star, bigger than all the rest and golden bright, rose above the jagged mountains at the valley's edge. From within the fortress came the sound of many voices chanting, and the tramp of many feet. With this sound came thoughts of a new danger. What would the consul do to him who had killed the High Priest? "Lord God, Almighty," Jared prayed silently, "do Thou save my friend, who slew only to save us both!"

Eben showed no signs of fear; he stood facing the portal; his lean bronzed face was lined and weary, but he did not tremble. If Eben could face death proudly, so could Jared. Jared did not think Jerah would hold him blameless in this death either. He wished he were taller; it was hard to act

the man when you were always singled out as the smallest
and youngest—was this not the very reason Uzal had picked
him for a sacrifice?

The chanting swelled; a long procession came from behind
the tower: the consul, the soldiers, the lesser priests and
temple attendants, and in their midst, Merbal, no longer
looking so sure of himself. In the orchards below the fortress, the birds were singing a hymn to the Morning Star
too. One column, carved with the star symbol, cast a long
shadow, like a finger pointing directly to the altar, and to
the body of Uzal lying in a twisted heap before it, with the
gold handle of the sacrificial knife protruding from his
chest.

The crowd gave a great shout. They will set upon us and
tear us limb from limb, Jared thought. The consul hurried
forward to examine the corpse. When he spoke, his voice
was shaken. "Not for many years has Uzal, the High Priest,
had the use of his limbs for walking. Yet when Attar summoned him, Uzal rose and bared his bosom to the sacred
knife. And those whom we bound upon the altar Attar has
set free. The god has spoken; Attar has had his sacrifice!
The strangers have come in good faith and said truly."

The temple attendants gathered round the body of their
leader and bore it away, chanting solemnly. Others came
with golden buckets to wash the blood from the stones. The
sun came up, flooding the courtyard with golden light. Attar,
the Morning Star, faded into the rosy sky. The night seemed
as if it had been a dream.

"All that you asked of me shall be given to you," Jerah
told Merbal. "It will take time to gather together a suitable
amount of gold; meanwhile you and those with you may
dwell among us in safety." He beckoned to an attendant and

pointed to Eben and Jared. "These two are the favorites of Attar. Bathe them and anoint them and dress them in fine garments. Tonight we shall feast together in honor of Solomon and great Sheba."

It was autumn before the gold shipment was ready, for now the consul was determined that King Solomon should receive only the finest of the products of Zimbabwe. Behind the fortress hill, there was a village where the soldiers and lesser officials lived, and here, to Jared's relief, the shipmen were quartered, instead of in the gloomy temple-fortress.

Below the temple, in the cellars, were the smelting furnaces and workshops where slave craftsmen fashioned golden bowls and pitchers, beads for necklaces, bangles of twisted gold wire, golden thread. Of all these the consul gave Merbal a store, as well as cakes and ingots of raw gold, and ivory horns filled with gold dust.

He would by no means permit the shipmen to carry the treasure back to the ship themselves as if they were common porters. That was a job for slaves. Jerah was plainly irritated by Merbal's crude manners, and so when it came time to select porters, Eben was asked for his advice. Jared also, in spite of his youth, was consulted. Ever since the High Priest's death, Jerah had showed these two members of the ship's crew special favor, a habit which Merbal bore with ill grace.

The slave quarters were circular holes only twice as wide as the height of a man, and three times as deep, built of granite blocks, with a tunnel entrance that could easily be guarded by a single soldier. In the bottom of the crowded pit the black men sat huddled with drooping heads. Only one, a giant in size, stood upright, staring at the bit of blue sky he could manage to see. It was Kalonga.

Jared nudged Eben. "There is the man who guided us here," Eben said. "Let him guide us back again to the port."

"He is not needed for the return," Jerah said. "The river will take you there."

"Then let him be one of the porters," Jared said diffidently. "He can carry a larger load than any of the others."

The consul agreed. Those selected were taken to a loading platform where the sacks and bundles of golden treasure were strapped upon them. Two Sheban guards were charged with watching them and bringing them back to Zimbabwe after they had discharged their burdens.

Because of these guards, Jared had no chance to speak to Kalonga on the road to the river. Just once he managed to whisper, without being noticed, "If I could only help to set you free!" Kalonga's lips silently answered that he understood.

The galley was in good shape and ready to sail, for the men aboard had been relieved several times and kept advised of plans by courier. The consul had sent plentiful supplies of fresh food, the produce of farms worked by slave labor in the valley of Zimbabwe. All the water jars were filled, and there was nothing now to do but load on the gold. When all was stowed below decks, Merbal was almost dancing with joy. As well he might be, Jared thought; at the risk of his own life and the lives of the crew, Merbal had finally got all the gold the ship could carry. But he too was happy, and so were the other shipmen. When they pushed the galley out into the river this time, they would know for sure that they were heading home, and nothing—neither storms, nor calms nor headwinds would keep them from reaching it.

The shipmaster was in such good spirits that he insisted on a noontide feast with the Shebans before leaving; indeed everyone was in a humor to celebrate. Only the black slaves had no part in the merriment; having finished the loading, they were huddled together under a tree. While the wine was passing from hand to hand ashore, and the meat was being prepared, Jared stepped back on board to find Methuselah. The monkey had made such a racket with his welcome to Jared that Merbal had ordered him tied to a rower's bench. It was stifling below, and Jared could hear him complaining bitterly.

The months of special treatment at Zimbabwe had made Jared bold and reckless. Anyhow, Merbal was too busy celebrating to notice if he slipped down into the hold for a moment to set the monkey free. He was busy untying the knots of Methuselah's halter when a hand grabbed his arm and another was clapped over his mouth. "Do not cry out; it is I, Kalonga. Save me as you promised, young comrade; hide me; take me with you!"

Jared knew he could not refuse. He could only hope that after the feast the Shebans would be too tipsy to count their porters, or to notice Kalonga's absence. Later, when Merbal discovered the stowaway, Jared would be in trouble again, but this was a chance he had to take. Now that he had his gold, perhaps the shipmaster would be less ill humored. Already he seemed so.

"Come," Jared said, "let us make a hiding place."

The whole forward part of the hold was bulging with cargo now. Hurriedly they loosed the awning which covered it, pushed aside chests and bales, and made a little cavern into which Kalonga folded his great length. Jared closed the mouth of the space with goods, and tied down the awning over the whole. "I will bring you food and water when I can," he whispered.

"Do not try," Kalonga said. "Gladly will Kalonga starve and thirst for a chance at freedom. Do not take the chance that I might be discovered till the ship is on the sea."

It was dangerous to remain here chattering, so Jared did not argue further. He hastily petted Methuselah, and left him, regretfully, tied as before. He could not risk the shipmaster's anger or suspicions by freeing the monkey now. He returned to the feast. No one had noticed his absence. The Shebans and Merbal had their arms locked in embrace; they were singing. So far, all was well.

CHAPTER FIFTEEN

Mutiny

FORTUNE was with Jared and Kalonga, for Merbal, flushed with success and wine, insisted on taking the galley out into the river directly after the feast, even though it was late afternoon. The Shebans roared goodby from the shore. The oarsmen, glad to be off, rowed with a right good will in spite of the heat. But soon, full of meat and wine as they were, they began to grow drowsy. Even Yshmael was yawning and slowing up the chant. Merbal rested on his cushions on the prow.

Jared, fidgeting each minute that did not put distance between the galley and the Shebans, scratched his head over what he could do to step up the pace. It would be of little use to seize an oar himself; one rower made small difference and he was still not one of the strong ones.

Eben was at the steering oars. The sun had set and the brief twilight would soon be followed by night. "Go rouse the shipmaster," Eben said. "It is time to pull the galley ashore."

"Surely it is not *yet* time," Jared said.

"Have you forgotten the first thing I taught you about the duty of a seaman—quick and unquestioning obedience?" Eben said sharply. *"Go rouse the shipmaster!"*

Still Jared hesitated. Should he risk his friend's anger? Or should he tell Eben of Kalonga, and why it was important to leave Zimbabwe behind as quickly as possible, and not to go ashore till the ship was well beyond reach of the Sheban slave guards? Close as he and Eben had grown, Jared was still not sure how the helmsman, with his stern sense of ship's discipline, would act about a stowaway. "The shipmaster gave no orders to rouse him," Jared said stubbornly.

"The shipmaster needs neither rousing nor advice!" barked Merbal's voice. "We will *not* go ashore this night. It is as easy to steer by the moon as by daylight, and the current will carry the ship downstream while the men sleep. If you have no will for this steering, give over the helm to Jobab."

"I have will enough," Eben said.

Merbal grunted and returned to his post on the prow.

"Forgive my disobedience," Jared said humbly to Eben. "I had a reason . . ."

"With such a shipmaster, who can keep order?" Eben growled. "I thought the time for taking risks was over, but it seems otherwise. Say no more, small brother. I do not blame you. Go to sleep like the rest." And to himself he murmured, "Why is Merbal still in so much of a hurry?"

Jared did manage to slip food and water to Kalonga when the galley landed and the men went ashore on following nights. Merbal had grown strangely careless of what the boy did. Hunched over the tablets where he kept his accounts, Merbal brooded on something. Eben also noticed this mood, but none of the others did, seemingly. The sky by day was sullen and the jungle as oppressive as ever, but the oarsmen rowed lustily, singing of home.

When they came to the mouth of the river, the galley

was drawn up on a sandspit far from the town. This night the shipmaster ordered all ashore except his cronies and himself. Jared sat by the cook fire on the beach with Eben. Across the bay the lamps of Tharshish flickered faintly. Jared was worried that Merbal would check his cargo before putting to sea, and would discover Kalonga. So far this evening the shipmaster had remained on deck with the others gathered around him, talking in low tones. Eben was staring up at the galley, and Jared whispered to him. "What are they doing there? Why did Merbal tell some to stay with him and others to go ashore? It looks like a council of war that Merbal is holding on the ship."

"A council on the weather, most likely," Eben said. He wet a finger and held it to the wind. "See, the wind is against us; it is blowing south. If he were to ask my advice, I would say we should put into the port till the monsoon changes."

"Why doesn't he ask your advice?"

"I am no longer in favor. If I disagree with him, Jobab will take my place."

"Jobab is nothing like so good a navigator as you!" Eben shrugged, as if to say, that had nothing to do with the case.

Merbal did not make for Tharshish next morning, but for the open sea. There was still a stiff breeze blowing from the north, and when he gave the order to set the sail, Eben looked startled. Jobab, who was at the helm, grinned slyly as a cat.

Merbal swung his arm and pointed. "South!" he said. And indeed with such a wind, the ship could have gone no other way. But the course to Ezion-geber was north.

"South!" Eben cried. "Does the shipmaster think there is yet more gold in the south? Do we not have enough and more than enough? The ship is already so heavy-laden that I fear for its safety in a storm."

"I have enough gold," Merbal said, "and this time I am going to profit by my trading."

"Merbal is driven mad by his gold lust," Eli muttered to Jared. "Do his words make any sense to you?" Jared shook his head.

"Do you think I have undertaken so many risks merely to fill the coffers of kings?" Merbal continued.

The other shipmen understood no better what Merbal was driving at. Questions broke out on all sides. "What of us? What will happen to us?" they asked suspiciously. "What of all the risks *we* took? What of all our labor? And what good does it do to keep sailing south?"

"You are simpletons," Merbal said. "Do you not see that there is plenty of gold for you to share in, so long as it is not handed over to Solomon?"

"But how can you do this without calling down the King's wrath upon us?" Peleg said. "And on yourself too?"

Merbal chuckled, pleased with his own cleverness. "Jerusalem and Tyre are not the only cities in the world where gold is power. The land of Africa must come to an end somewhere soon, according to Jobab. With this wind we shall sail round it into the Western Ocean and up the other coast to the Western Isles or some other pleasant land where neither the monarchs of Tyre, nor Israel nor Sheba have sway. There *I* shall live like a king—and you too, if you stick with me, can have everything your hearts desire."

"My heart desires home and my wife and children," Bela wailed. And Jared, not daring to provoke Merbal by crying out loud, choked at the thought of never seeing Judah again.

No gold, no comforts and luxuries in a far land would make up for the loss of home.

"Besides, who knows there is an end to Africa?" Bela quavered. "We might sail south and south till the ship drops over the edge of the world into an abyss!"

But there were still others, like Peleg, whose eyes gleamed with greed, and who cheered loudly for Merbal's plan.

The whole ship was in turmoil. Eben shouldered his way through the clamoring men to face Merbal. "*No*, shipmaster. This I will not do. Nor will the rest of the crew."

Merbal snapped his fingers. Kalab, Yshmael, Abu, and the others who had held council with Merbal the night before appeared suddenly at his back, armed with swords. "*I* am the master of this galley!" Merbal snarled. "The crew will do what *I* say! Only those who are loyal to me will share in the profits. For the rest it will be . . . !" He made a downward motion with his thumb toward the waves alongside. "Who dares to oppose me?"

Jared knew now that he should have told the story of the Queen's casket long ago, so that the men might have known how untrustworthy a shipmaster they had.

"If you go with Merbal," Eben said, "you will never see home or kindred more. You will lead the life of hunted outlaws. Merbal's way is the way of a bandit and a traitor!"

"And your way is the way of mutiny!" Merbal shouted. "The punishment of mutiny, as every seaman knows, is death!"

"Then it is mutiny!" Eben cried in a ringing voice. "Who will stand by me, for the sake of his own honor, and the King?"

Cowed by Merbal, none of the crew dared answer. Jared scrambled to the top of the merchandise piled on deck amidships and yelled, "Do not trust Merbal's promises; he is a liar as well as a thief! He promised the King that he would deliver a casket of rare jewels to the Sheban Queen; he is stealing that too. He will never give you the rewards he promised!"

But even those who were against Merbal's scheme were afraid of him. "Muzzle this midget-sized prophet!" Merbal said, and added in a scornful drawl, "I had thought to deliver the casket some day, but since it is no longer convenient, the jewels also will be divided among my loyal shipmen." He made a sign, and his armed guard, with Kalab at their head, moved forward. Both Eben and Jared were overwhelmed and hustled below. They were lashed with their backs to the foot of the mast where it came through the deck into its braces. Merbal promised them that as soon as he had time to spare from the handling of the ship, they would be punished as they deserved. Neither of them doubted that the punishment would be death. Only Merbal's haste to get away from the Sheban port was saving them for the moment.

Merbal kept the men at the oars all day, and when night came, he still gave them no rest. At the time of star rise, some of the oarsmen were replaced by deck hands, and Eli managed to get himself a place on the beach nearest the prisoners. But he did not dare to speak to them, for Yshmael, with whip and drawn sword, sat watching.

By turning his head, Jared could see Eben's face. When the ship rocked, a beam of moonlight from the open hatch flickered over it. Eben looked white and as though carved out of stone.

"Eben!" Jared whispered. "Do you wake or sleep?"

"I do not sleep." His voice was dreary, as Jared had never known it to be.

To cheer himself as well as his friend, Jared said, "We escaped once before—at Zimbabwe."

"Even your sharp teeth could not gnaw through this heavy coil that ties us," Eben groaned. "I have been stupid as an ox. Long ago I should have seen that to obey *this* shipmaster without question was disaster. Long ago I should have suspected his treachery. Many of the shipmen are loyal to the King. But they are afraid to stand against Merbal. Only you had the courage to take my part."

"Am I not your brother?" Jared said.

"You are, in all truth."

Jared fell into dozing and wakened again at the sound of scratching in the cargo behind him. Rats—big ones, by the noise they made. He was bound and helpless, and he shuddered at the thought of them. Then he heard a whisper, and knew, with a great lifting of hope, that it was not rats.

"Jared, do you speak?" Eben asked.

"No, it is Kalonga," Jared answered in a low voice. "He is hidden in the cargo." Eben's eyebrows shot up in glad surprise. He too felt there was hope in the unsuspected presence on board of the giant black man.

"My friend, you are in trouble?" Kalonga whispered.

"Merbal has made us prisoners," Jared said.

"Kalonga will set you free."

"Not yet," Eben ordered. "Wait—I will give you a signal when we have made a plan—when the time is right."

Jared did not think the time would ever be right for the three of them, unarmed, to overcome Merbal. But Eben was a better judge of the other shipmen's tempers than he was. The shipmaster had now kept them at work from sunrise till after the middle watch. And the crew were beginning to realize what it meant to be in Merbal's power. There would be no other justice to which they could appeal, ever. They were no better than slaves. Now the whip whistled on the back of every man who did not bend to his oar with all his might. And there was the armed guard to carry out more serious punishment if the shipmaster ordered it. The eyes of many an oarsman were fastened on Eben's face as if he regretted that he had not cast in his lot with the helmsman.

Jared grunted as the rope that wound round him and Eben tightened. Eben was straining against it, trying to hear something Eli whispered. A rising wind made the ship's timbers groan. The oars creaked in the rowlocks. Under the cover of these noises, Eben and Eli whispered to one another each time Eli leaned forward to make the start of his oar stroke. Yshmael, half asleep, took no notice.

"Keep up your hope," Eli said.

And on the next stroke, "Most of us are with you."

"Then rise against Merbal," Eben said.

"We do not dare," said Eli. "No arms—no leader."

Eben was silent for a few moments, thinking. He leaned forward again. "I have a plan," he said when Eli's face came close. "Pass the word back. The men must chant—loudly— to cover what we do here."

Eli nodded, turned his head to the oarsmen behind him; the word flew from mouth to mouth. Eli began to sing and the others joined him in an ancient chant of rowing men.

"What is the meaning of this?" Yshmael shouted, roused by the chant. "You do not need so much of a noise to row by."

"If the shipmaster forces us to work at the oars hour after hour in the dead of the night, we must sing loudly to keep awake," Eli said. Yshmael grunted his consent, surprised that the men could still have so much spirit.

The moon had set; it was dark in the hold now, and Yshmael did not see the huge black man, gaunt as a skeleton carved from ebony, make his way out from under the cargo cover. The swelling chorus of the chant covered the noise of the ripping awning. Crouching, threatening as a black shadow, Kalonga moved up the aisle between the rowers' benches. He pounced, and Yshmael slid from his seat without a sound.

"Keep rowing so that Merbal does not suspect!" Eli said. He seized Yshmael's sword and with a few hard slashes, severed the rope that bound Eben and Jared. "Will you try for freedom?" Eben asked the oarsmen.

To a man they nodded yes. "What shall we use for weapons?",one said.

"The oars," Eben said.

"Yes—the oars, the oars!"

"Come then, follow me," said Eben. He started for the hatchway.

The oars were so long and unwieldy that Jared could barely drag the one that Eli had abandoned to the deck. Here most of the men were asleep, and when Kalonga let out a blood-curdling war cry, they roused up in terror, thinking the galley had been boarded by a savage host. They found themselves surrounded by a horde of men flourishing long, stout cudgels. Those who resisted were knocked over the head. Eben took care of Merbal with a blow of his fist. Soon all the weapons were in the hands of Eben's followers, and the others, without leaders, begged for mercy. Kalonga, with a broad grin, planted his feet on the half-conscious shipmaster.

Eben sent the cringing Jobab to the steering oars. Then he held up his hand for silence. "We must plan what we shall do. The ship is without a master. Let any man speak who has a suggestion."

Eli, sword in hand, bleeding from a cut on the forearm, fiery·eyed, shouted, "Eben shall be our shipmaster!"

"Eben will take us home!" Jared cried.

The others shouted their approval.

"I will do my best to take you all safely to Ezion-geber if you will trust yourselves to me," Eben said. "Do not expect any miracles. There will still be winds that are against us. We have come a long way, and it will be many moons before we make our way back. Also King Solomon's gifts must be taken to Sheba, and the gold which is rightfully the Queen's turned over for fair apportionment."

This also the men agreed to, though with less enthusiasm.

"And I say we shall put Merbal to death before he causes any more trouble," Eli said.

"Yes, kill him! Kill him!" shouted the shipmen—those whom he had whipped, or kept at the oars long days and nights without rest.

"No," Eben said. "We will not kill the shipmaster. He must be brought to King Solomon's justice."

The crew muttered, angry; their thirst for revenge was a burning one, now that Merbal was helpless.

"If you wish to kill him, you will have to overcome me first," Eben said calmly. "And then you will have no one that knows the way of the winds and stars save Jobab. Do you wish him in my place?"

"No, no!" the crowd shouted.

"Bring a rope," Eben said to Jared.

When it was brought, Merbal was trussed hand and foot,

and thrown like a sack at the foot of the golden cargo that was his delight.

Though Jared also did not like killing, he would have felt far safer with no Merbal on the ship. But now Eben was the shipmaster, and his commands were law.

CHAPTER SIXTEEN

The Queen of Sheba

MANY months later the ship came again to the Red Sea. When Jared saw the mountains of Sheba, he felt that he was nearly home. Yet once this land had been the end of the earth to him.

He had learned much in the time that had passed. Eben still called him affectionately "small brother," but there came a day when—after Jared had been boasting a bit—Eben said, "You don't have to put on such a show of being a big fellow any more; we have only to look on you to know it." Indeed, his eyes were almost on a level with Eben's, and Jared knew that Shem would no longer be able to bully him. But it wasn't only in the matter of size that he had changed. What a child he had been on the night he had crept from his mother's dwelling place! Dreaming of lumps of gold, yellow as butter and shining like the sun! Well, he had seen so much gold that he was sick of the sight of it, and more than sick of the slavery that dragged it out of the earth.

Kalonga had been put ashore at a wild spot on the coast where there were friendly tribes and he was safe from Sheban slave masters. "If it had not been for you," he told Jared, "Kalonga would not have found freedom again. May you never lose yours." Jared did not fear to lose his freedom, for he knew that Eben would give the King a good report of his behavior. Merbal, it was true, still threatened punishment to those who had mutinied, particularly to Jared, for he seemed to feel that his downfall was as much due to the boy as to Eben. But Merbal was a prisoner, bound and tied; the King would not take his word against Eben's.

Eli thought Eben was too merciful to Merbal, as well as to the former shipmaster's cronies, Kalab, Abu, and the rest, who now claimed that they had been forced into doing Merbal's will.

"They are a danger to us," Eli said. "Why do you not put them ashore at some desert island if you will not kill them?"

"Because that is more cruel than need be," Eben answered. "Perhaps some of them did obey Merbal out of fear. Now they obey me because *I* am shipmaster. But I do not put any trust in them."

To Jared's disgust, Jobab, whom Jared trusted least of all, was still on board, but Eben promised to dismiss him as soon as the galley reached Sheba, his native land. The port of Ophir was made without trouble, and the harbor master gave permission to Eben to take gifts to Maraiaba, the Queen's capital city in the mountains.

While the ship had been forced to wait in an African port for favorable winds, Eben had searched it for the Queen's casket. It was not very hard to find, for it was merely shoved as far up in the hollow bow of the galley as possible and covered over with chests and draperies. Now it was taken out and loaded, along with some tokens from the mines of Zimbabwe, on the backs of donkeys. "I shall give the Queen an accounting of the remaining gold," Eben said. "It is too heavy to carry all of it on such a journey. The

Queen will decide what fair share goes to our King in return for the use of his ship."

"*We* underwent all the danger and labor of fetching it," Peleg grumbled. "Why does the Queen deserve any? She will never know what we have stowed below decks."

"I am not a thief like Merbal!" Eben snapped.

Eli was put in charge of the ship while it remained in the port. Eben instructed him to watch Merbal particularly. Jobab, for some reason, was reluctant to leave the ship, but Eben would not listen to him. He was sent away weeping. Jared and three others were selected to accompany Eben to the capital city.

"I trust these Shebans will not be so suspicious as those at Zimbabwe," Ira said nervously.

"Why should they be?" Eben said. "We have brought here the gold of Havilah of our own free will."

Jared was not afraid. He would have howled with disappointment if Eben had left him behind, for this was the land known as Ophir, the fabulous land he had so long wanted to see. Besides, the sight of the mountains made the very muscles of his legs ache with the anticipation of climbing to high country once again. The little caravan left the barren shore behind, crossed fields green with new barley, and followed a path beside a tumbling stream of icy mountain water. It was more delicious to Jared than wine. The Shebans were fine engineers; everywhere were cisterns and dams and canals, and as a result, the countryside was rich with plantations and orchards.

Soon they began to climb. The peaks ahead were sawtoothed and so high that Jared's hills of home would have been mere earth heaps beside them. When the caravan made camp at night, the others shivered, but Jared happily blew out his breath for the mere pleasure of seeing it once more issue like smoke from his mouth. His blood raced as it had never done on the hot and narrow deck of the little galley.

"The sea has its virtues," he told Eben, "and I no longer fear it more than it deserves to be feared. But how much more beautiful are the everlasting hills! Do you not ever tire of the ocean wastes, Eben?"

His big Tyrian friend looked into the camp fire a long time before he answered, "I have never known anything but ships and cities. The sea has been good to me; it has given me a livelihood and at times much pleasure. But I am growing old; it is a lonely life."

"Come to Judah with me," Jared said. "My home shall be your home. My mother Mara will welcome you as my brother."

"Perhaps I will do that," Eben said. "I should like to see the land of my own mother's people—the land of the people of Israel. According to your words, the Hebrews have a god and a way of life that seems better than those of Tyre and Zidon. But we have still to make the journey to Maraiaba, and back again, and the passage of the Red Sea to Ezion-geber. No voyage is over till it is over, nor should one count on safe return till the ship is finally at rest on the beach."

Jared lay by the fire that night wondering what had happened to his mother and to Shem in his absence. More than two years had passed—they might well count the youngest of the family as dead. Perhaps by now Mara had taken unto herself a new husband; Jared could not blame her if she had. Life in Judah was difficult for a widow woman, and Shem had never been the most thoughtful of sons. Jared remembered how he himself had sworn to bring back to Mara all the comforts and luxuries his toil could earn. So far he had nothing to bring her, but Eben would surely see that he got a fair share of the rewards for this voyage.

The journey to Maraiaba was long and difficult, for it lay far away and high above the sea on a plateau amid the mountains. Many days later Jared stood on a windy ridge looking down into a green vale filled with sunset light. The brisk air smelled of ripe and dropping apples, quinces, and mangoes. Blue shadows slowly mounted from terrace to terrace, blotting out the orchards and jungles of fern and wild flowers. A few fingers of rock, twined with creepers, still glowed ruddy pink. The sound of running water filled the valley; hundreds of little streams spouted from clefts in the rock, coursed down the mountainside or tinkled through man-made channels into a gleaming lake where the waters were trapped by a huge dam. By the side of the lake, in the midst of flower gardens, lay a palace of many colors, crowned with golden domes, looking, from this distance, like a gilded and jeweled toy.

The caravan descended to the city, where Eben presented King Solomon's seal and the letter which the King had sent with the casket. The shipmen were politely received and comfortably housed till they were summoned, some days later, to an audience with the Queen.

The palace, known as Dar Saleh, the House of Happiness, was a far cry from the gloomy fortress of Zimbabwe. It was all color and light, built of marble, carnelian, and delicately carved, scented sandalwood. In the vast council chamber, though it was noon, a thousand lamps threw their light up to the polished red ceiling studded with sparkling crystals. And a thousand warriors made a pathway through their ranks for the four shipmen carrying King Solomon's casket on their shoulders, and Eben marching at their head.

Blinking in the bright light, Jared saw at the far end of
the room a raised platform covered with soft carpets and
cushions on which reclined the Queen's ladies in waiting,
nibbling at sweetmeats from small golden tables. He lowered
his eyes, for the sight of so many jewels and bare shoulders
made his step uncertain. He had a moment's glimpse of the
Queen herself before he and his comrades laid down the
casket before her high throne and prostrated themselves in
the Eastern manner. She was the most beautiful creature
Jared had ever seen. She was extraordinarily tall for a woman.
Her skin was like dusky silk, and her eyes like black fire,
made larger with blue paint and a dusting of gold on the long
lashes. Her crown was of ruby flowers and emerald leaves,
hung with chains of gold and silver. Her gold-embroidered
leopard-skin robe swept to the floor. The chamber was heavy
with incense, but the Queen's perfume, like the night-bloom-
ing lily, drove all other scents before it. Jared was glad to
fall on his face; the scent made him dizzy.

"Bilkis, Queen of the South, greets the messengers of the
King of Israel." Her voice was husky and deep, but you
would never have mistaken it for a man's voice. "The letter
from King Solomon, which I have read, suggests that we two
make a league for mutual benefit. What think you, my counselors?"

The growl that issued from the Queen's advisors, massed
behind her throne, sounded far from friendly to Jared's ears.
He dared not look up.

The Queen went on. "King Solomon, who calls himself the
King of Kings, sends to me gifts and asks in return black
wood of ebony, red gold, and blue sapphires."

"This petty King is bold to the point of insult," said a man's
voice scornfully. "How long has his little kingdom existed?

Less than a hundred years. The Sheban lords have held sway over Ophir and the South for half a thousand years. And he dares to suggest a league, as between equals!"

These Shebans were not kindly folk, any more than they had been at Zimbabwe, Jared thought. Eben had been foolhardly to place himself in their power.

"King Solomon's kingdom is young, but it is powerful," the Queen said. "We have heard, before this, of his legions, of his horses, and war chariots. And, above all, we have heard of Solomon's wisdom. This is not the first messenger who has come bearing gifts from him. My lord Tamrin, my devoted counselor and friend, you who have been to the land of Israel and seen it with your own eyes, what do you say to this?"

Since Jared was prostrate, all he could see of the great merchant prince Tamrin was his solid-looking feet in golden sandals and the hem of a jewel-encrusted robe. "King Solomon is indeed wise. Because of this his people have peace. They are not divided by petty strife; they are loyal only to him and to their god. So the kingdom is strong and the King has alliances with many lands. My advice is that the Queen would do well to make a partnership with him."

The Queen's garments rustled as she moved restlessly. "King Solomon has bidden me to visit him that I may see the glory of his kingdom. Perhaps I will go there to test this wisdom of his. What else have you to say, shipmaster of Solomon? Above all, why have you taken so long to bring these gifts to me? For I see by the letter that it is over two years since you left Ezion-geber—a voyage that should take less than a moon. Are then King Solomon's ships so slow and feeble?"

"No, great Queen, they are sturdier and swifter than all

others," Eben said boldly. "We have only just returned from a voyage to the Queen's lands of the far South, bearing with us gold to the amount of many hundred talents, of which this is but a sample." He flung down an ivory tusk which he carried on his shoulder, and from its hollowed-out center, gold dust spilled like common dirt across the carpet.

"By what authority did you take treasure from my mines?" the Queen said furiously, and behind her the counselors shouted, "Thieves! Robbers! Put them to the death!"

Jared grew cold with fear, but Eben's voice was strong and unafraid.

"An overambitious shipmaster of Zidon, who is now a prisoner awaiting King Solomon's judgment, directed this venture. He had no authority but his own. But we overcame him and have brought an accounting of the whole cargo to await the Queen's pleasure."

Now Jared could hear murmurs of surprise and gratification from behind the throne. "Shipmaster," said Queen Bilkis, "you are an honest man! Had you stolen the gold, I should soon have learned of it, and there would have been bad blood, perhaps even war, between King Solomon's land and mine. But because you have dealt fairly, I will send to Solomon not only those things for which he asks, but all the gold which you have brought with you. Tell the King that if his ships are so sturdy, and his shipmasters so honest as you are, he and I together will make a mighty enterprise!"

Jared was filled with pride at the words of the Queen, at the thought that Eben and his shipmates had actually played a part in furthering the glory of King Solomon's empire and in keeping the peace between two great nations.

It took some time to load the ship with the presents which the Queen sent: the black wood, the blue sapphires, and two peacocks from India in cages, beautiful birds with harsh voices. Methuselah hated them and stood before their cages scolding busily, which only made them scream the louder. Again the ship was delayed by the winds, and it was autumn by the time it left the land of Ophir for Ezion-geber.

Homeward bound, Jared sang as he helped set the sail; the oarsmen sang at their oars. Even Merbal in his bonds was less abusive than usual, which seemed strange, since the day of his judgment was drawing near.

The ship was well out in mid-channel when Jobab appeared from a hiding place below. "Do not send me back," he pleaded, with clasped hands and large tears in his liquid brown eyes. "I could not stay in Ophir; the Sheban shipmasters do not like me."

Eli, furious that Jobab had managed to stow aboard, in spite of his watchfulness, said, "I wager I know why. They know you're not to be trusted."

"My comrade must not say such things," Jobab whined. "They are jealous—I know more of navigation than any of them."

"Perhaps so, but you will have no chance to show it on *my* ship," Eben said impatiently. "I do not wish to turn back, so behave yourself and I will let you stay."

Methuselah jumped to Jared's shoulder and pulled his ear, whispering in it. Jared wished he could learn the monkey's tongue as readily as he had learned others.

"The little ape behaves as if he has something to tell you," Eli said.

"I wonder how long Jobab was in the hold and whether he spoke to the prisoner Merbal there," Jared said. "Perhaps Methuselah saw them and heard what they said. Eli, we must keep our eyes on that tricky Sheban."

"And on Kalab and Abu and the rest of Merbal's friends too," Eli said. "They have a cocky look on them today. We must warn Eben of it. I do not like the smell of things this morning, for all of the fresh autumn breeze and the sunshine."

CHAPTER SEVENTEEN

The Stormy Wind

THE passage of the Red Sea was almost completed. Another night and day, from sundown to sundown, and the galley *Mekada* could rest her battered, salt-encrusted planks on the beach at Ezion-geber. Up ahead a short distance now was the entrance to the Gulf, marked by the cliff upon which Merbal had so nearly dashed the ship on the outward voyage.

Eli was at the helm and Eben stood beside him, searching the sky with narrowed eyes.

"Is there weather coming?" Eli asked.

Eben nodded. "I do not like the sultry look of those purple clouds over the mountains. There can be wicked storms here at this season, and the ship is so heavy laden she does not rise easily to the waves. Let us make for the islands this side of the point; there we can find shelter if need be."

But the storm pounced suddenly as a hawk from the sky. At one moment the islands were dark plums swimming in evening light; in the next they had vanished in swirling blue-black vapors, and a gusty wind flew across the sea. Night descended with the storm. The galley staggered sidewise as from the blow of a mighty fist.

"Take in sail!" Eben shouted. Peleg and Ira swarmed up

the mast and straddled the yard, reaching down to gather in
the folds of the sail as Jared and the other deck hands heaved
on the halyards. The ship lurched like a drunken man and
the lines were now tight, now loose. The mast whipped back
and forth as if it were a slender reed instead of a stout Lebanon pine. One of the brailing loops which gathered up the
sail snapped and blew free, snaking out on the wind and
leaving a corner of the sail to fill like a puffball.

Jared tugged at the lines with his eyes half closed against
the stinging spray. He did not watch what happened above,
and was suddenly knocked to the deck by the weight of
Peleg, who had slid part way down the mast and jumped the
rest. "The mast is breaking asunder!" he yelled. When Jared
caught his breath and looked, he saw how the stick was bent
in an arc by the pull of the flapping sail.

Eben roared at Peleg: "Back to your post, sailor! The mast
will break indeed if we do not take the strain of the sail
from it!"

But Peleg, cowering, would not go. On every man's face
was written the dread of being asked to take Peleg's place
and be tossed perhaps into the churning waves. Jared was
afraid too, but someone had to help gather in the sail; it was
heavier than Ira, up there alone, could manage. Jared had
climbed the mast often enough now to feel at ease in ordi-
nary weather. This was different, but he managed it, though
the spar was slippery with spume that fountained halfway
to the yard. Ira reached down a hand and helped haul him to
his dizzy perch. The ship did its best to shake them both
loose, but they locked their knees around the yard as it
swung through space, and reached for the sail as the men
hoisted it from below, inch by inch. The harsh wet linen tore
from their hands, but somehow they managed at last to

bunch it together and tie it round. Then they slid down again to the deck.

Now the bare-masted galley ran before the gale like a wounded animal, while the voice of the hunter yelled close on its heels. The terrified peacocks screamed fiendishly.

Each time the prow buried itself in exploding foam, the ship struggled less valiantly to rise. In the hold, water crept above the feet of the oarsmen. They crowded out on deck, adding to the confusion there.

"Get below and bail," Eben shouted. Jared and the others grabbed bowls and pots and dipped them up, full of water, bumping elbows, getting in each other's way, spilling almost as much as they managed to toss overboard. Eben ordered all but the oarsmen back to the deck. And still the water level rose.

"Our only chance is to find shelter before the ship founders," Eben said to Eli. "Have we steerage way?"

"A little."

"Then make for where we last saw the islands."

Jared could hear, above the screaming wind, a booming and crashing that could have been either thunder or surf. Eli heard it too. "What of the reefs?" he shouted.

"We must chance them," Eben said. He went to the prow to watch for the sign of white water breaking on rocks. All around was the blackness of night.

A blaze of lightning lit up the ship. Jared cried out, for in the instant of light he saw Merbal with a knife in his hand creeping towards Eben. Behind him came Jobab. Eben, staring out into the gloom, did not see them. Jared ran forward and made a flying leap for Jobab, crying out a warning to Eben as he leapt.

Wrestling with Jobab was like wrestling with the slimy

octopus of the sea. The Sheban's limbs gripped Jared like tentacles and there seemed no way to throw him off. Jared had grown strong for his sixteen summers, but not strong enough for this. Jobab pinned him down, and squealed with the laughter of a jackal. "So the little brother thought himself big enough to fight with grown men! That comes from Eben's pampering his conceit. It will be different for him when Merbal has the ship again!"

But Merbal must not have the ship again! Jared, writhing and struggling, could free himself only enough to watch what was taking place. Abu and Kalab had overpowered Eli; the steering oars swung wildly, unattended. All over the storm-tossed galley men were locked in struggle, Merbal's friends against those who were loyal to Eben. In the lightning flashes the ship glistened wet from stem to stern; every timber and rope was bright as silver. On the prow Merbal and Eben strained one against the other, the powerful, heavy body against the tall and wiry one. Lightning flashed on the long blade of the knife as Eben forced it from Merbal's grip into the sea. Slowly Eben was driving Merbal to his knees. Merbal wrenched himself loose and backed away, drawing closer and closer to the rail. Eben followed, and again they wrestled upon the slippery, heaving deck till Merbal lost his footing and staggered back, pulling Eben with him. Just in time Eben wrenched free, hung for a moment off balance, and stepped back to safety as Merbal, with a loud cry, plunged into the waves. A shout went up from the shipmen.

Jobab, watching too, had forgotten Jared. Jared gathered every bit of his strength and threw him off. Taken by surprise, Jobab rolled across the deck, bounced against the rail, and knocked himself out. Meanwhile Bela, the fat little cook, crept behind Kalab and hit him over the head with a heavy kitchen pot. That set Eli free to deal with Abu, who was soon begging for mercy. The ship was again Eben's.

But the storm, which had quieted a bit as if it too were watching the man-made battle, struck again in full force.

"Back to your bailing!" Eben shouted. Frowning, as he saw how deep in the water the galley wallowed, he said a moment later, "We must lighten ship!"

The men stood waist deep in water below decks, forming a line which passed up logs of ebony, ivory tusks, bars of gold —whatever heavy things they could get their hands on. Peleg groaned but Ira chided him. "Gold is commoner stuff than lives, isn't it?" On the top of the cargo pile crouched Methuselah, terrified and squealing, unable to escape because of the leash with which he was fastened. Jared paused in his work long enough to set the monkey free. Methuselah climbed on Jared's shoulder and clutched him round the neck like a frightened child; he was icy cold and shivering. "Poor little brother," Jared said, "we all forgot you."

The ebony logs bobbed away in the foaming wake; the gold bars sank bubbling. Only a small part of the gold was thrown overboard before the ship rode more lightly and took less green water over the prow. The bailers too made such headway that the oarsmen could return to their oars. Eben stationed Ira on the prow with the lead line.

"What depth of water do you find?" he shouted to him.

"Fifteen fathoms!" Ira sang out.

And a moment later, "Twelve fathoms!" shouted the linesman.

"Good," Eben said, leaning from the rail to see what lay ahead.

"Ten fathoms!"

A small rocky island, scarcely more solid than the giant waves foaming over it, loomed against the night.

"Let out the anchors, all four of them!" Eben ordered. "We may ride here in safety till morning."

The island gave a little shelter from the gale, though the *Mekada* still romped at the end of her anchor lines with timbers groaning. Jared eyed the toothed rocks of the shore and hoped he was a good enough swimmer to reach them, with Methuselah wrapped round his neck, if the ship, battered as it was, fell to pieces. One would have to be a strong swimmer not to be battered to pieces oneself upon that shore.

But the ship now seemed in much less danger, and the men, exhausted, dropped to the deck. The peacocks had stopped screaming, and the wind began to die down. Eben and Eli went over the vessel for leaks, tightening a brace here, untangling a mess of lines there.

"She is a stout ship," Eben said, as they came back to the poop deck. "There is some little water coming through a few seams that have spread, but these we have plugged with linen waste." He stood by the rail, looking up at the sky and out over the water to the island, which was gradually becoming more visible as the light grayed.

Jobab crawled to Eben's feet. There was a large bump upon his head which Jared viewed with satisfaction. "Master, master," the Sheban whimpered, "Merbal forced me to cut him loose. Do not hold it against me."

Eben kicked him away. "You should be tossed to the waves along with the others who smiled at me and schemed behind my back." He looked with distaste on Kalab, Abu, Yshmael, and the rest of Merbal's men, who crouched in a corner of the deck, wondering what their fate was to be. "But I am a shipman, not an executioner. You shall be bound and delivered into King Solomon's hands."

It was the moment before dawn. The clouds broke apart, showing red sky over the black mountain peaks of the land of Midian. The waves were gentling to long slow swells of shining purple. Eben ordered the anchors to be drawn up and the oarsmen to bring the ship in to the beach.

Jared stretched himself out on the sand, shivering in his wet clothes. But a glorious sun was coming up which soon would warm him and drive the aches from his weary limbs.

"We are all alive!" said Bela, as if surprised.

"All but Merbal, who has gone to his just punishment," Eli said.

It seemed very strange that Merbal should be dead. His going lifted a weight of dread that had hung over Jared for so long, and yet he could not rejoice in a death. Perhaps Eben was feeling the same, for he passed his hand across his brow and said wearily, "If it had not been for his greed, Merbal would have been a great shipmaster. We should never have reached such far lands nor brought such treasure to Solomon if it had not been for his boldness." He turned to Jared. "Will you do me yet one more favor, brother?"

"Gladly!"

"I am tired, but I can find no peace in my heart, no rest. I cannot drive away the thoughts of what passed during this night. Will you thank your god for keeping us safe?"

It was dawn, the hour of prayer. Jared too felt full of gratitude. When he had made his prayer, he took his flute and played upon it a psalm of praise. Then he sang aloud the words of it.

They that go down to the sea in ships, that do business in great
    waters;

These see the works of the Lord, and his wonders in the deep.

For he commandeth, and raiseth the stormy wind, which lifteth up the waves thereof.

They mount up to the heaven, they go down again to the depths: their soul is melted because of trouble.

They reel to and fro, and stagger like a drunken man, and are at their wit's end.

Then they cry unto the Lord in their trouble, and he bringeth them out of their distresses.

He maketh the storm a calm, so that the waves thereof are still.

Then are they glad because they be quiet; so he bringeth them unto their desired haven.

CHAPTER EIGHTEEN

A Mighty Treasure

AND so at last Jared came to the place he had set out to find almost three years before—Jerusalem, the city that was the center of the center of the world. The crew of the *Mekada* had been summoned to appear at the court of Solomon.

From afar Jared spied the citadel, a crown of saffron-colored stone on the brow of Mount Zion. The shipmen followed the camels, heavy laden with the ship's cargo, along the black basalt highway to the Valley Gate in the south wall. Jared drew a deep breath of wonder as they entered the narrow, climbing streets.

The King received them in his great audience chamber, where a forest of carven Lebanon cedars upheld the lofty roof. The magnificence of this chamber was hardly less than that of Maraiaba, but Jared gave it hardly a glance. He was unhappy with the thoughts that had been coursing through his head all the way from the seaport. The smell of the copper refineries at Ezion-geber had reminded him all too vividly of life in the King's mines. Solomon's palace smelled sweetly of incense, but Jared could not get the stench of slavery out of his nostrils. He did not fear for his own freedom, however, for Eben would give a good account of him, and surely King Solomon would take Eben's word over that of Kalab and the others who marched roped to one another with chained hands.

Solomon sat on his jeweled throne surrounded by his queens and the elders of Israel. The shipmen marched the length of the hall and set down at the foot of the throne the bundles of ivory and spices, the gold, silver, and jewels.

The astonished murmurs of the court were loud as the wind in the forest. The younger among the queens twittered like birds, pointing to the peacocks in their gilded cages, and Methuselah, perched on Jared's shoulder.

But King Solomon frowned when his eyes fell upon Eben, clad in his simple worn tunic of white linen, at the head of the column of shipmen. "Where is Merbal, the admiral of my navy?" the King demanded.

Eben bowed low and handed up to the King a clay tablet. "Merbal is dead, my lord. Here on this tablet is inscribed all that happened, and an accounting of your ship's cargo. I am Eben, my lord's servant, and I await his judgment."

King Solomon studied the document in silence, and for many minutes a leaf could have been heard to fall in the audience chamber. Jared trembled. What if the King, after all, did not believe Eben's account?

At last the King raised his eyes from the tablet and fastened his glance, keen and fierce as an eagle's, on Eben's face. Eben did not blink nor falter, for he had nothing to hide. "It is well," the King said at last. "You have dealt bravely with one who would have betrayed me. And not even the sea lords of Tyre and Zidon have ever sailed so far or brought back such a fortune as this I see before me. The other three ships of my navy did well, but nothing like this. Now indeed my treasury will be filled to overflowing. And even greater than these is the deed you have done for Israel in cementing our friendship with the Sheban Queen."

Kalab, dragging the other prisoners with him, plunged to the fore, fell on his knees, and held up his chained hands. "Justice, my lord; I cry for justice! Do not believe the words of this man Eben, who mutinied against our rightful master, Merbal, and murdered him for profit!"

"Silence!" The King's voice would have turned anyone less bold to stone. "Do you think I cannot read faces as well as words? What mutineer and murderer would dare to come willingly before me? What thief would bring to me such a treasure, accounted for down to the last penny?"

Kalab cringed. Solomon ordered his guards to remove him and the other prisoners. "These men will receive their just punishment. It is a pleasanter duty for me to reward those who have been loyal." He told Ahishar, his chamberlain, to give a purseful of coins to each of the crew.

Jared received his with misgivings. This was the wage for which he had toiled long and hard, the gold he had left home to seek. Now he could purchase at least some of the gifts he had promised himself he would bring to his mother Mara. But the clinking purse gave him little pleasure. He sighed heavily, and Methuselah, noticing his gloom, tried to comfort him with shrill, cheerful chattering.

"I see that you have brought us an ape from the far-off lands," Solomon remarked to Eben. "It is a rare beast, precious as rubies, and will afford my court much amusement." He beckoned Jared to come forward, that he might view the monkey closer. The other shipmen fell back; Jared was surrounded by emptiness on every side. He made an awkward bow, with Methuselah clinging to him. The monkey pointed at Solomon's blazing jewels and squeaked loudly. A titter, quickly hushed, ran through the crowd; a guard stepped up and reached out for the monkey. Jared knew the moment had come to part with his pet, but he could not help resisting, till the guard took the monkey roughly from his arms. Methuselah wept.

King Solomon looked Jared up and down till the boy's very ears grew crimson; his knees had long since turned to jelly. To Eben, Solomon said, "I remember this youth. He came to me for judgment at Ezion-geber, before my navy set sail. It is a bold youth that dares to speak his mind to the King. Sometimes that is a bad thing; sometimes a good one. You, Shipmaster Eben, must give me your report on him. Was he brash and impudent, questioning your orders? Or did he carry out his duty?"

"None better, my lord," Eben said. "The ship and all in it would have been lost if it had not been for the lad's quickness and courage only a few days back."

Solomon nodded, and said to Jared, smiling, "You are no longer the little he-goat I knew, but a youth who carries himself with pride. Even then I thought you would do well, but I wished to hear it from your master in words. Now what does this young shipman ask as his reward?"

In spite of the King's graciousness, Jared's voice cracked as it had not done for a long time as he answered, "My lord promised his servant freedom from slavery."

"You have kept your bargain and freedom is yours," the King said. "Freedom is a great thing, surely, but since you have done more than your duty, you shall receive more than freedom as reward. Will it please you to receive a second purse of gold?"

It was a tempting offer, but somehow he could not accept

it. What then should he claim as reward? There was a long silence in the hall, broken only by the frightened twittering of Methuselah. The monkey, held prisoner by a soldier, had his paws before his eyes and his long tail drooped. Jared's throat tightened at the thought of losing him, even though he knew that Methuselah, as court pet, would not be mistreated. Dared he ask for so precious a reward as this valuable beast? Already the queens were pointing to their new playmate and whispering their delight to one another. Stammering with fear at his own boldness, Jared said, "I—I should like to have the ape!"

The King gave a ringing laugh; the most beautiful and richly dressed of the queens smiled and nodded. Solomon motioned to the soldier, who loosed his hold on the monkey. Methuselah ran on all fours to Jared, jumped to his shoulder, and hugged him round the neck so tight that Jared was near to choking. Again the ladies of the court tittered.

"Never have I known one who preferred an ape to gold," King Solomon said. "Never have I known gold to be refused save by the holy men who dwell in the wilderness and think only on the Almighty. Has the boy Jared become such a one?"

Jared shook his head dumbly.

"Why then?" The King pressed him for an answer.

Jared fell to his knees. "Do you think me ungrateful, my lord, or overbold. It is only that I have seen how Sheba's slaves toiled for this gold, and I do not long for riches dug from the earth with such suffering. At Ezion-geber, the King of Kings said that some day perhaps slavery would vanish from the world. This is what I hope and pray for."

King Solomon sighed. "Ah yes, I remember; it was thus also you spoke of slavery then. Perhaps this gold will bring no blessings to my kingdom, and the ape would have given me more pleasure than riches. Perhaps in this you are wiser than King Solomon, whom people call the wisest man on earth.

"And now, Shipmaster Eben, what shall *your* reward be?" the King continued.

"Your servant needs no more than his just wage for the work of the voyage, my lord," Eben said.

"I am fortunate in having such servants as the brave shipmen of my navy," King Solomon said.

And now it was spring again, and Jared lay on his back under the old olive tree. His knees were crossed and one dangling sandaled foot kept time to the tune he was piping. It was spring in Judah; the new grass was sprouting, thick with red anemones and crocus; the corn was thrusting spears of green through the ruddy earth, and the terraced fields soared up to a bright blue sky where the clouds were white as new-washed wool. In all the villages men shouted and sang for joy in the spring, even as the psalmist wrote.

It was good to be home. His mother Mara had embraced him with tears and rejoicing. "I have brought a guest," Jared had said, motioning to Eben, who stood by his side, tall, bronzed, and shy as a boy before woman. Mara, still slender and graceful as a girl, had run to fetch water to wash the dusty feet of the travelers.

Shem had given Jared a boisterous welcome and said, "I am glad you are grown to a man's size and can do a man's duties. For I am taking to myself a wife in the next village, and I must go to help my father-in-law with his spring planting." So Shem had left Mara's house, and Eben, quite naturally, had taken to sharing the work of field and pasture with Jared. The Tyrian had a great zest for it, as if after all the years at

sea, he was starved for the sight of green things growing. This season the widow Mara would have a fine harvest.

In the branches of the old tree, there was a scampering and a squeaking that a bird never made, and an olive of the previous year, dry and hard as a nut, hit the top of Jared's head. He sat up, frowning in mock anger at the wizened little face peering down at him from among the gray-green leaves. "Behave yourself, Methuselah," Jared scolded, "or I shall not take you with me to guard the flocks any more." Methuselah would never make a shepherd, that was certain.

At the sound of Jared's scolding, a kid that had been eyeing the monkey uncertainly, bounced off to join old Navi and the rest of the flock, which were scattered over the hillside. At the foot of the slope, Jared could see Eben and Mara, their heads bent over a sapling pomegranate that they were planting. Jared smiled with content.

Some while after Shem had gone from the household, Jared had said to Mara, "Have you forgiven my wickedness in running away without your blessing, my mother?"

"Since you have returned, there is nothing to forgive," Mara said.

"But I brought you back so little in either gold or gifts!"

"You have brought me a treasure far rarer than gold," she said.

He had not known then what she meant. It was later that she and Eben had told him of their great happiness. For Mara at last had found a man she would joyfully take as husband. And Eben had found a woman to love, a desired haven after his lonely wanderings.

Someday when he was fully grown, Jared knew he too would find a wife to cherish. Meanwhile he would gladly bide with these two. He wanted to roam no more. He had

journeyed across the sea with King Solomon's navy, and he had learned much; but the hills of Judah held everything most dear to him.

He looked down again at Eben and Mara and his heart grew warm and happy in his breast. Friendship and love— that was what he had brought back. It was a mighty treasure.